*f*P

His

INSIGNIFICANT

OTHER

A Novel

KAREN V. SIPLIN

The Free Press

New York   London   Toronto   Sydney   Singapore

THE FREE PRESS
A Division of Simon & Schuster Inc.
1230 Avenue of the Americas
New York, NY 10020

For information regarding special discounts for bulk purchases,
please contact Simon & Schuster Special Sales:
1-800-456-6798 or business@simonandschuster.com
Designed by Karolina Harris
Manufactured in the United States of America
10 9 8 7 6 5 4 3 2 1
Library of Congress Cataloging-in-Publication Data
Siplin, Karen V.
His insignificant other : a novel / Karen V. Siplin.
p.   cm.
I. Title.
PS3619.I65 H57 2002
813'.6—dc21
2002016468
ISBN 0-7432-2278-4

Acknowledgments

Major thank-yous to Elizabeth Kaplan, Dominick Anfuso and Kristen McGuiness.

I am also grateful to the members of the John Oliver Killens Writers Workshop, whose critique never fails to astound, whose support is priceless.

For offering their home as a sanctuary from noisy, upstairs neighbors and permitting me to write in peace, I thank Carol Dixon and Jude-Laure Denis.

Thanks to the members of the New York Celebrity Assistants, a fabulous group of people, whose enthusiasm means so much.

Support, understanding and positive energy are important ingredients in the recipe for a writer's success. So, loads of love and gratitude and positive energy go to early champions of this book: Andrew Davidson, for coming over on a Sunday (no questions asked) and reading the book from beginning to end without complaint or judgment. And to Scott Chayet, for reading and making me laugh with every e-mail and phone call, and for just being so darn cool.

For being a truly extraordinary boyfriend and human being who paid the rent, fed me and patiently read version after version of this book, I thank Harris Schwartz. You are wonderful and beautiful.

A world of love and thanks to my sister, Alice, who bought me my first computer and never expected me to do anything else but write. To my parents, Robert and Helen, for supporting me for so long in every way, and never once asking why. I would not be who I am without you.

for my family

for Harris

for my uncle, Jesse James Evans (wish you were here)

Love is a dog from hell . . .

—CHARLES BUKOWSKI

His
INSIGNIFICANT
OTHER

One

I was waiting for something to happen and it didn't, so I fell asleep in the big green chair in my living room while the television was blasting and the lights were out. I could have been dreaming; I don't remember. I just remember sensing her presence, smelling her scent, feeling her arm brush past my face. Of course, the sound of the television being turned off woke me up, as well as the total darkness disappearing into light.

And she was there.

Mali was returned.

There's a reason for everything. I've been taught to believe that. But there are still plenty of things I can't explain. I can't explain why zebras have stripes. I can't explain why people are so complicated. And I can't explain why Mali returned. More significantly, I can't explain why she returned to me.

At least I couldn't then.

"You should never fall asleep in a chair like that," Mali said and I jumped. "Eventually it'll ruin your back and you'll get osteoporosis ten years earlier than you were supposed to."

"How did you get in?" I asked, staring at her like she was mad. My boyfriend's ex-girlfriend, all six feet of her, was looming over me, telling me what not to do.

"Good question," she said.

"Would you like to answer it?"

"It wasn't locked, Casey."

I hadn't locked it.

"In this day and age I'm fascinated by anyone who would leave their door unlocked, anywhere. I know this is supposed to be a safe building and all, but even in safe buildings rape happens. I mean, for God's sake, one of your neighbors held the door open for me."

It only happened once, he'd said.

Shit.

The sight of her standing next to me, sporting dark glasses and a mop of curly, black hair, was shocking. Her years of training as a classical ballerina were still at work: she stood upright and tall, feet spread shoulders-length apart. She was thin and had great muscle tone. She wore no makeup, yet her skin was bright, even and clear. I thought: She's not beautiful. He must know she's not beautiful.

"What time is it?" I asked, standing up. It didn't help. She was still much taller than me.

"A quarter past midnight. Were you waiting for someone?"

She knew what I was waiting for: I was waiting for the phone to ring, I was waiting for him to call and say he was running late, I was waiting for him to open the door with a bouquet of fresh roses and a bottle of Piper Heidsieck champagne.

"Yes," I said. "It's our anniversary."

"Oh?" She tried to sound surprised, but I knew that tone of voice. It was the trying-to-sound-surprised-and-bored tone of voice. Who did she think she was kidding?

Mali Bengoechea was the girl my boyfriend made mad-passionate-love to for four years before he made mad-not-as-passionate-love to me. It was her job to know what night it was.

They say there are few guarantees in life, but when you're a woman on the verge of turning thirty, there are several. Without fail, a gorgeous woman will always manage to introduce herself to your boyfriend at a party the very minute you stick a chicken wing in your mouth. The part of you that turned off the telephone ringer and lowered the volume on the answering machine just to have a couple of hours to yourself will disappear and you'll want to talk to the man in your life, whether he's special or not, every minute of the day. And the moment you and your boyfriend reach a significant milestone, like an anniversary, a woman from his past is sure to reappear. Women love men who aren't available. It makes the chase more challenging.

That's where women like Mali come in. The best friend of twelve years who never found him attractive until you came along. The woman at the bar, the party, the wedding, who thinks he's cute and doesn't care that you're standing next to him, your arm through his arm; she just has to get a number out of him, or a smile, before the night is over. Or simply the ex who wants to give it one last shot.

"Where is he?" she asked.

"Not here," I said, glancing at the nearly empty bottle of Chardonnay I'd been drinking while I waited for him to remember, the Chardonnay that had put me to sleep. Mali looked at the bottle, too. And she smiled.

Three months earlier, I'd learned Mali slept with my boyfriend during our nine blissful months together. *It only happened once,* he said. In a moment of sheer drunkenness, weakness and stupidity, it only happened once. That was supposed to make me feel better. It didn't.

For a while, I refused to see him. I wouldn't take any of his calls. I spent weeks feeling betrayed, like there was no reason to trust anyone ever again.

But I didn't break up with him.

I tried to figure out why I couldn't find the courage to do it. I'm no idiot. I'm a teacher, for God's sake. I spent seven years in a great university and thousands of my parents' hard-earned dollars to learn how to solve complicated problems. So, why couldn't I toss this guy aside and find solace in a few good affairs of my own?

Simple. I was holding on to my man with a desperate intensity I never thought I was capable of because I didn't want to wake up one morning and realize I was thirty and single. He could have fucked the entire Yankees baseball team and as long as he didn't dump me, it would have been fine.

Actually, there was more to it. After a succession of boyfriends who came too quickly and thought women's lib meant the woman should pay for everything, there was John Paul. He picked up the tab without the blink of an eye, sent cards when he missed me, and rubbed my back in the middle of the night if I couldn't fall asleep.

He was my first *real* boyfriend and I loved him. I didn't want to lose him to anyone. Especially not Mali.

I wanted to win.

"I'm sorry to put you in this position," she said.

"What position?" I asked, keeping my guard up.

"I'm in a bind. I really need a place to stay."

"You can't stay here," I blurted.

She considered my answer for a minute, and then she said, "Can I have a glass of water?"

I stared at her, surprised that she wasn't trying to convince me to give in. And then I moved toward the kitchen.

"And John Paul's number," she added. "He changed it since I left."

I stopped, hesitated, shivered, and then asked, for lack of anything better to ask, "How do you take your water?"

"Tepid," she said.

Every woman deals with the news of an affair differently. Some women drink. Others eat. I became celibate.

John Paul handled our "situation" like a perfect gentleman. He never complained, never threatened to leave me, and if he slept with another woman before Mali returned, he never told me.

The *Oxford American Dictionary* defines *celibacy* as "the unmarried state." There is no definition for it in the *Scholastic Children's Dictionary*. And stated simply in the *Longman Dictionary of American English* are the words: "not having sex, especially for religious purposes."

And as I stood in my kitchen holding a glass of tepid water, I wondered if there was a definition for the moment when I was about to give up celibacy and was smacked in the face with the ex-girlfriend instead.

You see, I had the perfect anniversary gift in store for him; it was wrapped in a black teddy, covered by a short black dress. There was also a lifetime supply of extra-thin condoms from

Costco, which I thought would add that special something to the evening in case he didn't get the significance of the black teddy. It had been three months since we'd had sex, and the end of my stint as a celibate was my gift. I wanted it to be special.

If exes aren't good for anything else, they're good for ruining a very special evening.

She was standing in front of a bookcase I'd bought with John Paul a few months earlier, skimming through a book.

"Can I borrow this?" she asked without looking up.

"What is it?"

I went to her and stared at the book in her hands. It was a hardcover, first-edition copy of *Dispatches,* signed by the author, Michael Herr. My dad cherished that book, which served as his main source of inspiration while filming his Vietnam documentary *Khe Sahn.*

"Sorry, I don't loan signed hardcovers," I told her.

She flipped to the front of the book to check the signature, and then continued to skim through it without commenting. Then she put the book back on the shelf and looked down at me.

"Oh," she said. "My water."

She took the glass from my hand and walked past me, into the kitchen. I watched her sit down at the table and sigh heavily, like she'd really been through some terrible ordeal.

She drank the water in one swallow, closing her eyes.

"Perfect," she said. "Thanks. I was so thirsty. You should always drink water at room temperature. It helps you move your bowels. Cold water is a shock to the system. I don't know why more people don't know that."

"Can I ask you something?"

"Ask me anything," she said.

"Why are you here? Really."

"I was in the neighborhood," she answered.

"Why?"

She stared at me for a minute. "I just got back into New York." She pointed to her suitcase in the hall. "I was going to stay with a friend on Tenth Street, but she isn't home. Actually, she's out of town for a couple of weeks, according to her neighbors. You live a few blocks away."

"The train is two more blocks away," I said.

She sighed. "Can I stay one night? I just spent all of my cash on a cab from the airport and it's starting to rain."

I stared at the telephone and tried to think of a mutual friend who wouldn't mind a late-night houseguest. I came up empty. And at that moment, I saw no way out of letting her stay. As stupid and masochistic as that sounds, it's true.

"I know what you think about me." She sliced into my thoughts. "But it only happened once."

"You know what? That doesn't make it less deceitful . . . or awful."

She stared at her hands. "I know that. And I wish I could have been there when he told you. I wish I could have told you myself, so you would have known how sorry I was."

Casey, pay attention. This is what a duplicitous bitch sounds like.

"The night John Paul and I broke up," she said, "he took me out to dinner. We saw each other every day for three months after that. It wasn't healthy. We weren't together, but we were never apart. As much as I wish we could change how close we are, I can't."

"How could you come here?" I asked.

She stood up, annoyed. "Do you think I'd be here if I didn't have to be?"

"I'm not sure," I said.

"This isn't about you," she snapped. "You're the only other person I know in Brooklyn and it's late. I need a place to stay."

"This isn't it."

"*Jesus.*" She flushed. "I just need a place to crash. It only happened once. It's over."

I thought of the reasons John Paul was still worth fighting for. There were the superficial reasons: his face, his hands, his teeth, the way he held my hips and guided me when we used to have sex.

And there were other things.

I remembered the time he gave me a sterling silver watch from Tiffany's for my birthday. It was a replacement for a watch I'd foolishly left in my office overnight. The watch meant everything to me, simply because it belonged to my grandmother; it was irreplaceable. I'd taken it off to wash my hands and was distracted before I could put it back on.

Mali graciously offered her services and helped John Paul search for a watch just like it. And then she found the perfect substitute, and John Paul gave it to me on my birthday.

I almost smirked. Mali had the kind of chutzpah I envied and, this is the part I hate to admit, I still *liked* her. A little. To be honest, I'd never stopped. Not even when I hated her.

"Everything's so complicated," she said. And then she checked her watch and yawned. "Can I have John Paul's number? It's late."

I stared at her. People come between you and the one you love if you let them, if you believe you aren't worth getting anything worth getting.

I couldn't let her call my boyfriend. I knew he would let her stay at his place. He'd stay with me until her friend came back, but I would still feel insecure. I'd rush home every day to get his end-of-the-day call, just so he could never say, "I called and you weren't home, so I stopped by my place to pick up a few things and we started talking blah, blah, blah." I imagined there would be that inevitable night when he wouldn't make it to my apartment at all, and I would call and call until I reached him. He would deny everything I accused him of and I would never really know if he was telling the truth.

It wouldn't be pretty.

"You're right," I said. "It's late and you'd have a forty-minute ride into the city, at least. You can stay here tonight."

I expected her to smile that smile a woman smiles when she knows she's played you like a piano. But she didn't. She looked genuinely grateful.

And it was settled. She was staying.

Two

I was having drinks with Peter and Gabriella at Maddalena's the night I met John Paul and Mali. Peter and Gabriella were a supercouple. Peter was a bond trader at Morgan Stanley, and Gabriella was an aspiring actress. They were the kind of couple that people were in awe of because they were always laughing and finishing each other's sentences. They were the kind of couple that made people feel a tinge of jealousy because couples like that existed.

It was this one night, after knowing them for six months in the sole context of having-a-drink-at-the-bar-in-Maddalena's, when Gabriella turned to Peter and said, "You know who Casey is perfect for?" And Peter said, "John Paul!"

John Paul was Peter's roommate and close friend, and they were meeting him that night. It's nearly impossible to turn down a meeting with the perfect guy when the perfect couple is setting it up, and when the perfect guy is on his way over. Besides, Gabriella told me, Peter never introduced women to his buddy. *So I must be special.*

When I met John Paul I couldn't figure out why Peter and Gabriella thought we'd match. He was tall and handsome, charming and successful. He had deep brown eyes that were wide and attentive, a smile that could light up a room, and a laugh that was contagious. He was definitely out of my league.

And it's not that I'm ugly or flawed. I'm not.

I have a pretty but sad face. I once dated a guy who said he loved me because I always looked like I was about to kill myself. One guy at a party handed me a drink and told me to cheer up because I was ruining his buzz. I'd been having the best time of my life.

I'm neither rich nor successful, but I have a decent bank account. I'm not charming, but sometimes I make people laugh. I wear black clothes, not because they're cool or artistic, but simply because black is slimming. I guess what I'm trying to say is, when it comes to types, I didn't think I was his.

He was standing at the end of the long mahogany bar with his arm wrapped tightly around a woman's waist. From the looks of her, and how tightly his arm was wrapped around that waist, I could tell he liked them tall, thin and Latin. That should have been the first omen. And even from behind I could tell by their trendy, expensive clothes that they were a type of cool I could never be, even if I wanted to.

I concluded John Paul was probably the only black man Peter and Gabriella knew, and I was the only black woman they knew, and BAM! We were perfect for each other. When he looked at me, my feelings were multiplied. It wasn't even like he was looking at me so much as looking through me.

I was flattered that Peter and Gabriella thought I was a match for a "catch" like John Paul Waters, who could just stand a certain way and take my breath away, but it was also a bit depressing. He summed up everything I thought I could never have.

"I bet you're Casey," he said nonchalantly. Then his eyes faded away the way a man's eyes will when he wants you to know from the start that he's not interested. The woman he was with came over and smiled down at me, and John Paul introduced her as his girlfriend, Mali. I wasn't as shocked as Gabriella and Peter, who knew Mali as John Paul's friend but had no idea she'd recently—that afternoon—been upgraded to girlfriend.

I was disappointed. The perfect guy, it turned out, had already found the perfect girlfriend.

I started to feel sorry for myself as the night wore on. I was in the mood to meet someone attractive, and I wanted that someone to be attracted to me. I was also sorry for Gabriella, who felt obliged to sit by my side and tell me all of the things John Paul would have told me if he were interested. For instance, he worked in advertising and hated it, and loved rowing and hated basketball. Useful information for the woman in his life, but not for me.

Eventually John Paul stood next to me without his girlfriend and ordered a drink. He told me there was a woman at the end of the bar who had the best pickup line he'd heard all week. She said she wanted to teach him poetry.

"Well," I said, finishing my very weak Fuzzy Navel and shrugging. "Why does she want to teach you poetry when you already are?"

John Paul stared at me for a long time. The eyes that had faded away moments before came back and were suddenly seeing me. He started to laugh. It was a laugh I wanted to hear over and over again, a laugh I could fall in love with.

He said, "That's the best pickup line I've heard all year."

It was the start of a beautiful friendship. John Paul laughed at all of my jokes and loved chopped liver on bagel crisps and ate ice cream out of the carton. He was funny and smart and attentive to everyone around him. And after four years, I considered him one of my closest friends.

I knew his relationship with Mali was rocky when he started to show up to movies and dinners and Maddalena's without her. And then he would stay near a pay phone all night and call until he reached her. She was having personal problems, he explained vaguely. Nothing to do with them. Peter, Gabriella and I weren't sure if we believed him. He always refused to go into detail.

Mali broke up with John Paul a few weeks after their four-year anniversary because she *needed space*. I was glad. I knew John Paul could do better. Mali was a self-involved know-it-all who spent endless amounts of time talking about yoga, tai chi, and her body. And she was aggressive. I often wondered if she really loved him. If she could love anyone other than herself.

I wasn't surprised when John Paul asked me out on a date six months later. We had become close over the years. And I knew he loved me as much as I had grown to love him. Our friends said, as tricky as it was, it was okay. She dumped *him*, after all. And six months had passed without any signs that she wanted him back.

Still, I avoided Mali as much as I could during the first couple of months John Paul and I were together. I thought he did too. We heard tidbits about her from our friends—where she'd been seen last, and with whom—and I watched John Paul to make sure he didn't seem too interested, too curious.

When it was no longer practical to turn down invitations to the same parties Mali was invited to, we started to see her

again. And she was cool. She didn't hold a grudge. She was
nicer and more helpful than she'd been before she dumped
him. But somewhere inside of me I knew her smiles weren't
genuine. From the corner of my eye I would catch her looking
at me.

After a while, she started to call me. She invited me to the
movies, loaned me books she enjoyed. I forced myself not to
suspect anything when she asked how life with John Paul was
going, when she remembered his quirks and laughed too loud
when I confirmed they still existed, when she asked me if I
loved him and lost her smile after I said I did.

And I did love him. So much that I suffered from an attach-
ment to him that was so intense I lost a part of myself.

I didn't begin to hate John Paul—in the way only someone
who loves a person can hate that person—until it became clear
he still loved Mali. And when my hate for John Paul surfaced,
so did my distrust for women.

I showed Mali to my parents' old bedroom and she remembered it. I searched my brain for the time I'd brought her in
there. We shared a look and she smiled, and I thought better of
asking her what the hell that smile meant. Some things are better left unsaid.

"How are Mom and Dad?" she asked.

"My mom and dad? Fine."

"Still liking L.A.?"

"I guess. They're still there."

"I can't remember which soap your mother is in. I'm always
meaning to watch it, but it slips my mind. I'm not much for
television, unless it's something like PBS or Bravo. They air
ballet programs occasionally and that's a treat. I remember

your mom is very beautiful. Right? You look nothing like her."

"Gee, thanks."

"Oh my God, I didn't mean it that way," she stuttered. "You are both beautiful in your own ways. You look like your dad, who is a very attractive man. Your mom looks like Lena Horne and you . . . don't look like Lena Horne. You look like Lisa Bonet."

"I look nothing like Lisa Bonet."

Mali considered then nodded. "Maybe Nia Long?"

"You know what? Let's just say I look like me. That's easy. I look like Casey."

"Okay. You look like Casey. Whoever that is."

She laughed and winked at me, and the wink made me wonder what secrets she knew. I went to bed and I listened to her walk around the room down the hall. I listened to my parents' drawers being pulled open for inspection. I listened to her settle in.

I wondered if she dreamed.

How can you dream if you have no conscience?

The most important thing, I told myself, was that John Paul was in love with me. If he wasn't, he would have left me the minute I said I was taking away his privileges. That's how we work. Everything revolves around sex. Until you find the one person you truly love.

My friend Dock is the perfect example. He's one of those very eligible bachelors in New York City who doesn't have to have a great job to keep the telephone ringing. He has that much sex appeal. He works at Bobo's Southern Café and Bar on Ninth Avenue. He doesn't make a lot of money and he lives with his uncle, but the minute women spot him standing at the podium under the dim, sexy lights while Sade sings in the background, the rules that apply for most men are dropped for him.

Dock is sex. He oozes sex from his long, thin dreads to his manicured hands and feet. He can make you feel like you're the only person he woke up to see. Women know they aren't getting a silk scarf from Henri Bendel for their birthday, and they certainly won't be dined at the River Café on any occasion, but it doesn't matter. They know they will get great sex.

When Dock wants to end a relationship, all he has to do is invite her over, rent a movie, bring in take-out from Bobo's and not touch her the entire night. Some women think it's a fluke and hang around for a second night of this charade, but generally the answering machines are rolling when Dock calls a chick after one night of this.

Polo was different.

Polo Roth was a successful lawyer in her father's law firm and Dock was in love with her. He spotted her one evening at the bar and he had to have her. I was home for that call. He described every detail about her from his podium at the front of the bar: tall, sleek and sexy, an Asian beauty.

In the beginning, Dock and Polo had sex every day. He was totally gone over her. He'd call me every night, and we'd compare notes about what she'd said and how she'd reacted to an innocent comment he made. Then the day came when he said he was in love with her. Even I was scared. Dock never fell in love with any of them.

He had to give her the test. After a week of bad movie rentals, late-night take-out from Bobo's, and no sex, Polo was still answering her telephone. She'd even called and invited him to dinner.

That's how it works.

Sex, or the lack of it, weeds out the losers from the keepers. So John Paul was a keeper, right?

I sat up in bed and decided I had to run the whole Mali

thing by Dock. But the problem with calling Dock these days was Polo.

Unfortunately, Polo the Asian beauty turned out to be a Korean nightmare. She was demanding and possessive and very insecure. She blamed all of her character flaws on the fact that she was adopted and raised by an overbearing Jewish father and a neurotic Catholic mother. She was insecure because she had an identity crisis.

And if that weren't enough, she was a thirty-five-year-old single woman who worked at her father's law firm. What man in his right mind would ask out the boss's daughter?

Before Polo, Dock and I spent several hours a day on the phone dishing out the daily gossip about our friends and commenting lazily on the sitcoms we were watching at the moment we were watching them. After Polo, we spent ten minutes on the phone, tops, while he was at work.

This is an emergency, I told myself. I need to tell a friend.

Polo answered on the first ring and said, "It's after midnight."

"It's me. Casey. I'm sorry to call so late, but I wouldn't call if it wasn't an—"

"I know you can afford to stay up late when you *teach*." She made *teach* sound like a dirty word. "But I'm up at five, sometimes earlier, and the sound of a ringing phone bugs the hell out of me after ten."

"Is Dock there?" I asked, ignoring her speech.

There was dead silence on the other end. I knew I was wrong. I wouldn't want a woman calling my boyfriend after midnight. I also knew she wasn't going to let me talk to him. She wasn't even going to tell him I called.

Luckily, he was awake and grabbed the phone before she hung up.

"Casey?"

I was really happy to hear his voice.

"I have to tell you something," I said.

"Shoot."

I told him about Mali. Dock knew Mali and John Paul through me. Over the years we had developed a tight clique. Dock seemed to enjoy them, but when the cards were on the table, I knew he only considered himself *my* friend.

I could hear him getting out of bed as he listened. I imagined Polo's dark eyes following him out of the room until she could no longer see him.

This will not look good on my résumé, I thought.

"Throw her ass out," he whispered into the phone fiercely after I explained.

"I can't just throw her out."

"Why not?"

I didn't want to tell him about the scenario I'd created in my mind. No matter how much of a best friend he was, he was still a man. I didn't want to be slapped in the face with that typical-male-silence that comes once you've said something typical-female-paranoid.

"You know you can't prevent something that's destined to happen," he told me when I didn't answer.

"What the hell does that mean?"

"You know what it means," he said. "If you tell her to leave, she'll stay at John Paul's place. But you and I know if she stays at your apartment, whatever's going to happen is going to happen there."

That's Dock. Completely honest. You have to be when you only have five minutes. There's never any time for BS. But I hadn't called because I wanted a solution to the problem. I knew if I allowed Mali to stay with me so that she wouldn't stay with John Paul, the day of reckoning would still come. It would just *come* in my apartment. I called because I needed to tell a friend.

Most of the time I don't want solutions to my problems. I just want to tell someone. I just want to know someone's listening.

"Can she stay with you?" I asked.

"It's not your problem where she stays," he said. "Don't you know that?"

I did, and I didn't. "Can she?"

Dock chuckled. "I have to go, baby. Keep your chin up."

He hung up the phone.

Three

My mother, Linda Beck, is a soap opera actress. She plays a nanny on *Bright Horizons,* a six-year-old soap on cable television. She isn't terribly famous, but she is beautiful. When she lived in New York, I never trusted anyone who asked me out on a date because they usually wanted to have a glimpse of my mother. She lives in Los Angeles with my father, Bill Beck.

Dad is a documentarian. He made one widely acclaimed documentary, *Khe Sahn.* It won several awards but wasn't nominated for an Oscar, which he's *still* bitter about. And though "guest lecturer" isn't a job per se, Dad made it into one.

They aren't superrich, but they managed to send me money to pay maintenance on the co-op. And I wasn't an adult with a silver spoon in her mouth. The apartment was theirs if they moved back to New York. I was just a squatter.

My parents are graduates of Columbia University. They had

aspirations for me to go to Princeton or Yale, which is where Mom dreamed of going but didn't get in. I had difficulty explaining that I wasn't planning to leave New York. So I didn't. Columbia University was the only school I applied to.

When I was accepted, no one had a hard time believing it had more to do with my parents' fame and alumni status than my academic ability. I was insulted when my high school friends didn't congratulate me, when they all acted like they knew I would get in.

I didn't do well in school. I wasn't cut out for all of that time behind university walls. But everyone has to choose a career. I didn't want to end up doing something I wasn't completely excited about, so I chose film. The joke was on me.

In film class I felt incompetent. I couldn't figure out how to use a light meter no matter how many people explained it to me. And editing was a mystery. I was useless on the Avid Editing System. I spent hours at home studying, to no avail. The one thing I thought I could spend my life doing, I didn't get.

I came out of Columbia with a degree in film production and a couple of very bad scripts. I refused to move to the West Coast with my parents because I was one of those die-hard New Yorkers who would not be caught dead in L.A. I was determined not to lose myself in superficiality.

Instead, I remained grounded and unsuccessful in New York. I became an adjunct film professor in a school not worth mentioning.

Introduction to Cinema was my first class on Thursday. I was up early and I was tired. Mali had been in the apartment for almost eight hours. I'd barely slept. I called Gabriella and left a message that Mali had spent the night with me, was still sleeping in my parents' bed, in fact. Would Gabriella be up for a houseguest?

She picked up the phone just as I was about to hang up. "You're kidding, right?" she said drowsily.

"I'm not."

She was silent. And then, "Sorry. I don't think I should touch this one."

I took a deep breath. "You're not actually touching anything. She needs a place to crash for a couple of nights. Her friend is coming back soon."

More silence. And then, "No. And why are you helping her in the first place?"

"She doesn't know I'm helping her."

"*Oh.* I see."

"Do you? You don't think I'm crazy?"

"I think you're crazy," she said. "But I would probably do the same thing. Call me again if you really, *really* can't find anyone. But I'm not promising anything."

"Can you think of anyone else she can stay with?"

Gabriella sighed. "I'll try to think of something. I'll call her."

"I owe you one," I said, relieved. Gabriella usually came through.

I had my reservations about leaving Mali in the apartment alone, but I was late for work, and as long as I'd known her she'd never been a thief. Well, not where material possessions were concerned.

I left a note on the kitchen table telling her that I'd set the door to self-lock, and I decided to be positive. Gabriella would think of something.

After my first class I went to a greasy diner five blocks away from school because my favorite coffee shop, the Polka Dot

Puppy, was crowded with students I didn't want to see. As a student I spent my time dodging teachers, and as a teacher I spent my time dodging students.

I ate a toasted bagel with butter and jam and drank two cups of coffee. I stared at my notes for the next class, but nothing registered. I wanted to go to sleep. As I was about to take a quick trip to the pay phone to call Gabriella, I noticed the fireman walking toward me.

Firemen are the hottest men in uniform, hands down. I've always adored them. I don't know if it's the hat, or the black jacket with yellow stripes, or the boots. There's something about a man who shoots out of bed at the sound of an alarm and doesn't get cranky but dressed in less than thirty seconds to save lives.

So, when this fireman walked toward me, his eyes focused solely on me, I knew something was very wrong.

My office is on fire, I thought.

I imagined all of my papers, bits of screenplays I'd never bothered to put on disk, up in flames.

I stared at him, too petrified to move.

"Casey," he said. "In class you told us to call you Casey."

"Class?"

"Yeah. Hi." He held out his hand. He had strong hands. "I'm Josh. I'm in your Contemporary Directors class. At two."

"Oh. Josh," I said, standing. I smiled despite the slight resentment I felt for being disturbed by a student. A student who was dressed like a fireman, no less. A fireman, a cold bottle of Veuve Clicquot champagne and a weekend in a suite at the Peninsula Hotel is my biggest fantasy. And this fireman looked like the type of student I could touch without having a lawsuit filed.

"Please, don't get up." His smile was uncertain, like he

wasn't sure if he should stay or go. I touched his hand, letting him know he could stay. He stepped back, taking his hand with him, and I almost apologized.

I sat down again, motioning for him to sit with me.

He declined with a shake of his head. "Got some buddies waiting for me."

Outside, I noticed the fire truck.

"But, yeah, I'll sit for a minute," he said.

There was something familiar about his eyes, which were blue and intoxicating. I could never forget a pair of eyes that stared at me so intently. But that was all. Nothing else rang a bell. Not his thick, black hair or full lips. Not his name or his strong hands.

"I'm sorry," I said. "But I can't place your face. I bet you don't hear that too often."

He looked a bit shocked but covered it quickly. I realized he was the type of fireman who didn't know what he had going for him.

"No," he said quietly. "Not too often. I bet the same goes for you."

"Flattery won't improve your grade."

"I better remember that." He smiled. "Maybe a bottle of wine will."

There was always a little sexual electricity between my students and me. Electricity I liked to play with vaguely. Kids are attracted to young teachers. It makes the idea of crossing the line with an authority figure more attainable. But while the electricity existed, students hardly came on to me. There was the occasional attempt at eye contact, a hand lingering on mine when an exam was turned in. Nothing extreme. I never knew if it was because film students think they're just too cool for that kind of shit, or if my students thought I wasn't worth the trouble. In any case, nothing ever happened that I couldn't handle.

"Persichetti," he said. "My last name. I don't know if that helps."

"It doesn't."

"Then maybe my number will."

He said this very seriously and I wasn't sure if I was meant to laugh. He took a matchbook out of his pocket, which I found ironic, and wrote his number on the flap. He held the matchbook out to me, but I only stared at it.

"Oh shit," he said, noticing the look on my face. "This isn't a come-on."

"I didn't think it was."

"No? Oh. Okay." He didn't sound like he believed me, but he didn't pursue it. "I had to switch a few days with someone. His wife's pregnant. And, you know, we work twenty-four-hour shifts."

"No, I didn't know that."

"Pain in the ass, but it's pretty much the best way to get through a breakup. Four years and suddenly . . . well, you don't want to hear about that."

"Not really," I said.

He grinned. "Didn't think so."

"Well." I shrugged. "You're off the hook. I won't penalize you for missing class." Attendance wasn't a big deal to me unless a paper was due, and even then, a student could drop the paper in my mailbox before the weekend. The less I saw of my students, the better.

"Okay," he said just as one of his fellow firefighters walked into the diner and motioned for him. He stood up.

"Would you mind telling me how you found me here?" I asked.

Our eyes locked and it seemed, suddenly, like he was nervous.

He raked a hand through his hair and spoke self-consciously. "I . . . actually, I usually see you at the Polka Dot around this time."

"Oh."

"Figured I'd take a chance and try to catch you there. A few people said you stopped in and left. When it gets really crowded, I come here too."

"CD students go to the Polka Dot?"

"Yeah. Always. It's the unofficial campus coffee shop."

"Jesus, I better start going somewhere else," I said, truly horrified that I was a regular at a campus coffee shop, and that my students were noticing me and I wasn't noticing them.

"That's cute," he said quietly. "The way you call it 'CD.'"

I'd never heard one of my students describe anything I said as "cute." It was strange.

"But you can't stop going to the Polka Dot," he continued. "We love seeing you there. It comforts us in a way."

"Don't tell me that," I said. I hated the idea that I was comforting people without meaning to comfort them.

He smiled. He had a great smile.

"If I miss anything important . . . would you?" He put his fist to his ear to resemble a phone and left before I could tell him no.

The key to surviving high school and college is finding the right clique and latching on to it. To know you'll always have someone to meet you in the morning before class, and during the day between classes, is a relief. It's the same when you're teaching. Academic departments can be hell. It's good to have an ally to bump into when a department head or fellow professor is hassling you.

My only friend in school was Ariadne Cohen. She was an associate professor in the English department, not a lowly adjunct like me. Most of the time we got together to commiserate about our departments and the people we worked with. Ariadne would tell me about her colleague who mailed his students' stories to magazines without telling them because their rejections made him feel better. I'd tell her about my very married colleague who was always kissing students in the editing room.

She was waiting for me outside of my classroom, looking more like a student than the tough-as-nails English professor that she was. Ariadne is short and cute and black with a penchant for all things secondhand and classic. She spends hours at garage sales and consignment shops searching for clothes. In her fifties-style glasses and vintage clothing, she's like a throwback from an era we weren't even born in. In school, though, she has to be a little more conservative. In black suits, she is somber, tough, searing. Despite her toughness, she's warm and caring; she's the type of person you want on the other end of the phone when you're in a crisis.

"So," she said when she saw me. "Why didn't you tell me?"

"Tell you what?" I asked.

"She answered your phone."

"She answered my phone?" For a second I felt out of breath.

"You don't even let *me* answer your phone."

"You don't ever come over."

"If I make it a point to come over, will you let me answer your phone?"

I didn't say anything. I didn't think it was funny. Mali was still at the apartment. She was answering my phone.

"Why is she there?" Ariadne asked.

"She isn't supposed to be there . . . now."

"Why was she there before?"

I wanted to avoid the question and her tone of voice and her penetrating eyes. I wanted to avoid the next few seconds with her. But she leaned in close to me, expectantly.

"Because," I answered, staring back at her, defying her to tell me I was weak and I was wrong.

She didn't. Instead, she said she was going to stay out of it and let me make my own mistakes. She always said that, but she never let me make my own mistakes.

"Why don't we talk later?" I said.

I tried to enter my class but she blocked my entrance. A few students looked up and watched us, curious. Ariadne closed the door.

"Talk to me," she demanded.

I slouched against the wall and stared at my shoes. I didn't want to talk. I didn't want to feel the disappointment I felt. I wanted to have the previous night back, so I could lock my door.

"I know what's going through your head," Ariadne claimed.

"I thought you were going to stay out of it."

"You think you're in control if you know where she is. If she's with you. But you're giving her power by letting her stay."

I sighed and looked Ariadne in the eye. "I couldn't let her go to him last night."

"How do you know where she was going to go?"

"I knew," I said. "And it was raining. It was late."

"Have you called him? Have you talked to him about it?"

I shook my head. I hadn't called him. I was so focused on *her,* contacting him hadn't crossed my mind. And though forgetting things like holidays and birthdays wasn't unusual for John Paul, it wasn't like me to let him get away with it. But there was the Chardonnay, I reminded myself. And the unexpected sleep. And her.

"I wasn't prepared," I said.

"Prepared? What does that tell you? You think something might happen."

"Yes," I said. "Frankly. I do."

"You don't trust him."

"I don't trust *her*."

"You think something could happen. It's this celibacy thing, isn't it? I knew it would lead to something like this."

"Like what?" I snapped. For the past three months, since I'd told her about becoming celibate, Ariadne mentioned it every day. Everything that went wrong in my life went wrong because I was celibate.

"Like insecurity, fear. You need to ditch this celibacy act and fuck somebody. It doesn't have to be someone you love. And please don't let it be John Paul. Just fuck someone, already."

"Very nice," I said as a student walked between us and into the classroom. "Now my students know all about my sex life."

The thing about best friends is they don't care where you are when they tell you what's on their mind. Ariadne's like Dock in that sense. No matter where we are, I'm bound to get an earful about what I should be doing with my life.

"Sorry," she said. "You know I can get carried away. Everyone knows about it anyway."

She was right. My celibacy was like that old shampoo commercial with the blonde who says, " . . . and I told two friends, and they told two friends, and so on, and so on . . . "

"I just don't think you should end your celibacy with an asshole."

Asshole had become the primary word Ariadne used to describe John Paul since I'd told her that he cheated on me. But John Paul wasn't an asshole. I wouldn't have fallen in love with an asshole. Your friends only know what you tell them, though.

And I wasn't the type to call Ariadne every time John Paul left a white rose in my mailbox with a note that said he was missing me. We never announce the good things in our relationships because we don't want to brag. Telling another woman how great your man is just isn't something you do, either. So we usually tell our friends the bad things and later, it's all they have to work with.

"We make each other laugh," I said quietly, almost to myself.

"But what good is he if you don't want to have sex with him? What good is he if he hasn't tried to change your mind yet?"

"I don't know," I answered impatiently. Any other day I might have given the question more thought. It was a good question. But it was ten minutes after two and I was late.

Ariadne nodded and looked thoughtful and I hated when she did that. It was like she was saying she would always know the answers before I did because she was that much smarter.

"I have to go." I opened the door to my class. "Are we on for Friday night?"

"Always," she said as she walked away.

Four

I couldn't keep Mali a secret from John Paul. And I didn't want him to find out from someone other than me. I decided it would be less stressful to just tell him that Mali was back in town and happened to be at my place. The act of telling him and being completely stable and nonchalant about the whole thing would prove what the black teddy and condoms were supposed to prove the night before. I trusted him; I'd forgiven him.

I called him at his office and asked him to meet me at Maddalena's after work. Promptly he said he couldn't and I reminded him about our anniversary. He apologized profusely, admitted it had completely slipped his mind, and promised he'd be at Maddalena's by five-thirty.

John Paul was slouched in our regular booth, drumming his fingers on the table, waiting. When he saw me he sat up and flashed his good-to-see-you grin and I remembered another reason why I wanted to keep him. It was that front tooth that was kind of crooked that made him look like he'd been breaking the rules all his life, and that left eye that sloped downward when he smiled.

He stood up and kissed me and said, "Sorry about the anniversary."

There were already two beers on the table and a plate of Maddalena's wings. He grabbed the bouquet of white roses lying next to the beer and handed them to me.

I smelled them and sat down across from him. "I have something for you, too," I said.

I took the box of condoms out of my bag and put them on the table, next to the beer, next to the roses. John Paul stared at them, and then he looked at me.

"What . . . ?"

"Part of your anniversary gift," I told him, feigning sweetness. "Too bad you missed it."

He picked up the box and read the label. "Do I get another chance?" he asked.

"I don't know." I took the box out of his hand and put it back in my bag. "It's a gift I give only on special occasions."

He grinned. "Okay," he said. "I'm sure I can find some special occasion coming up this weekend."

Our waitress placed a grilled chicken sandwich in the middle of the table.

"Has your husband ever missed an anniversary?" he asked her.

Our waitress smiled a lopsided smile at John Paul. "Yes," she said.

"Do you let him make it up to you?"

She laughed. "He makes it up to me. If he knows what's good for him."

John Paul looked at me, his eyebrows raised, and then he looked at our waitress again. "Think we can have another plate?"

She nodded and he winked.

Our waitress blushed as she walked away. Waitresses were always blushing in John Paul's presence and John Paul was always winking at them, taking them into our confidence. He didn't even know he was doing it, actually. It was natural for him.

He sat next to me. "I'll make it up to you." He kissed the back of my neck, my weak spot. I felt a warm, fuzzy feeling inside of me that only girls in high school should feel. "Dinner . . ."

" . . . bubble bath . . . " I added.

He kissed my neck again. " . . . condoms. You and me."

We laughed. I bet a million people, men and women included, are stayed by the words *I'll make it up to you* every day. I closed my eyes and let him kiss me. I almost forgot about Mali.

Our waitress brought us an empty plate and John Paul stopped kissing me to glance at her. "Thanks. A few more napkins?"

I moved away from him and he watched me.

"I'm sorry," he said. "You want to ditch this place and—"

"We need to talk," I interrupted him, suddenly serious.

"Okay." He picked up a knife and started to cut the sandwich. Our waitress returned with a stack of napkins and he smiled at her again. "How's the baby?" he asked.

"Great," she said.

"You look good." He looked at me. "She has a baby at home. Three months old. Three months, right?"

Our waitress nodded, pleased that he remembered.

"Jeez." He shook his head. "If I could look that good after having a kid . . . "

She laughed. I smiled. "Need anything else?" she asked.

John Paul shook his head, taking another sip from his beer. He put half of the sandwich on my plate, licked his fingers. "You okay?" he said.

"I want you to *not* see her," I said, knowing perfectly well how impossible that was.

"Who?"

"Mali. She's back. She stayed with me last night."

He frowned at me. His eyes asked why I would make up such a sick joke. Then they clouded over as he stopped seeing me, as he realized I wasn't joking at all. "You're kidding." He tried to sound bored.

"No," I said.

"So you're not okay?" he said.

"I'm not sure."

He took a bite of the sandwich and watched me closely while he chewed. I wanted his sympathy or empathy. Anything. But he raised his eyebrows and spoke with his mouth full. "This is *fantastic*. Eat yours."

John Paul never spoke with his mouth full.

"I'm . . . concerned," I said.

He swallowed, tilted his head and asked, "Why?" in an I'm-here-for-you-if-you-need-me voice. He never did that kind of shit.

I wished he had reacted naturally. I could have handled natural. I could have handled a discussion about the fact that he still cared. I could have handled a discussion about what to do

next. And at that moment I realized I was afraid of my relationship with him. I was afraid because I couldn't control him.
Not that I wanted to control him. Or anyone. I just . . . I
couldn't control his beauty, or the way it drew women to him. I
couldn't control the eye contact, or the way women smiled
when he acknowledged them. And I wondered what good I
was if I wasn't in control.

"Sometimes I wonder if you know you'll never be loved by
Mali the way you're loved by me."

"Casey." He sounded touched. "Mali isn't a problem."

I wanted to believe that.

"I meant it when I said I don't want you to see her," I added.

His face darkened. "You can trust me," he said. "I don't want
to have to say it anymore. I'm tired of proving myself because
of one stupid mistake."

He said it in a way that made me never want to make him
say it again.

He finished his half of the sandwich silently. I finished my
beer. He stood up to pay the check.

"You want to wrap any of this stuff up?" he asked.

"No," I said.

I stared at the table, at the uneaten food that could have fed
a few kids in rural America. But I only thought of Mali, and
how she was always there. Between us. Bits of her. I didn't
know how to tell him that I felt that way because there were always moments like that one, when I wasn't sure he knew I was
there because her name had been mentioned.

He watched me walk over to him and he smiled distractedly.

"Is she at your place now?" he asked.

"Probably."

"It's nice of you to let her . . . be there."

"She was my friend, too."

He nodded, possibly remembering the time he and Mali helped me paint my kitchen, or the time the three of us rented a car and carried a picnic to Woodstock.

"Why don't we go back to my place?" he suggested. "I'll make last night up to you."

I didn't think it should be that easy. Because he would see her. Eventually. Maybe they'd run into each other at some museum or party I'd decided not to go to. I wanted to be there for their first meeting. I wanted to know when it was happening.

He put his hand on my back and I stiffened.

"Casey," he said, pushing me gently toward the door. "You're making me nervous."

I took his hand as we went outside. "Maybe it isn't me who's making you nervous."

His fingers slipped through mine. "Who else would it be?"

"I don't know," I said. "Why don't we go to my place and find out?"

He stopped walking. "What do you mean by that?"

I said, "You're trembling."

I put my hand on his chest and felt him tense. His reaction made me uneasy. He stepped back, stared at me.

I said, "You know you have to see her."

He looked away, and then he took my hand and held it, and we walked in silence toward the train. Before we reached the station he stopped, shook his head.

"I'm not going to do this," he said. "It doesn't make any sense."

He let go of my hand.

"Maybe I should see her alone first," he said.

"Why?"

He shrugged. "Forget it. I'm tired. I'm going home. You're sure you don't want to come home with me?"

I thought of that ridiculous quote about loving someone and setting them free, and what was supposed to happen if they loved you back. Did it even make sense?

"Go. See her alone." There was insecurity in my voice. "Don't keep anything from me."

He smiled softly, kissed my hand affectionately. I went back inside Maddalena's, ordered a margarita, and sat at the bar. The bartender stared at me curiously, but he didn't ask. I was glad he didn't ask.

His hands shake as he opens the door. He can't believe he's finally going to see her. It's been a long time.

She's standing in the middle of the room, waiting to greet me, waiting to say what she's rehearsed all day: I shouldn't have come, and I'm a selfish shit, and I'm leaving tonight. *When she sees him, not me, everything she's about to say washes away. It disappears.*

He grabs her, hugs her tightly, doesn't let her go. Then he covers her face and neck with kisses.

She laughs and tries to return them, but he's too excited to let her get anything done.

Finally, she pushes him away.

"Hungry?" she asks and I'm not sure if she means this literally or in some perverse way. It doesn't matter. He ignores it.

He says, "You're fucking beautiful."

She looks surprised and pleased. "Thanks. Where's Casey?"

"You're fucking beautiful," he repeats.

Now she's annoyed. This is something she never liked about him. And she never did take compliments well. "Okay," she says, as though the conversation will end sooner than they thought.

"Damn." John Paul looks around my apartment as though it's

different now that Mali's in it. "How was your trip? What are you doing here?"

"Needed a place to crash." *Mali picks up the beer she was about to drink when she heard the front door open. She takes a swig.*

"Here?" *he says, almost impressed.* "You have balls."

He's right about one thing.

Mali laughs. "You want a drink, Paulie boy?" *It's the nickname she gave him that stuck. Everyone calls him that. Including me. Only I say it along with a ruffle of his hair, just so he knows it belongs to her.*

"Yeah, I'll take a beer," *he says, grinning.*

Mali can't help but smile. She shakes her head, then gets him one.

"You're really hot," *he says, but she shrugs this off.*

He takes a cigarette from the pack on the table, and she lights it for him. They attempt to catch up.

Five

When I walked into my apartment there were three empty beer bottles on the living room table, as well as one glass and an unopened bottle of wine. I stared at the water rings on the table. It was antique, oak, expensive.

"What the hell are you doing?" I asked loudly, picking up the beer bottles and inspecting the rings on the table. "You have to respect my stuff."

Mali came out of the kitchen, wiping her hands on a dish towel.

"Oh, sorry," she said. She wiped at the rings on the table and I brought the bottles into the kitchen, washed them out and dumped them in the recycling bin under the sink.

She watched me as I checked my answering machine and jotted down my one message from Paul Zabrowski, the head of the film department at school. A department meeting was scheduled for the next day and I was required to be there.

"Where's John Paul?" I asked.

"You tell me," she said.

I looked at her. I didn't believe he hadn't stopped by.

"There were like five hang-up calls," she informed me testily. "That would drive me nuts."

I lowered the volume on the answering machine.

"Don't listen to my messages," I said. "And you don't have permission to drink my beer. And wine. You don't have permission to touch anything in this apartment."

The telephone rang.

"I'll replace the beer when I have some cash," she said. "I didn't have money to go out and buy anything."

I went into my bedroom and closed the door. I wasn't about to offer to loan her money.

"It's me," John Paul said.

"Where are you?"

"Home."

"Oh," I said.

"It doesn't make sense that she's there," he told me. "Why don't I stay with you tonight? She can stay at my place."

"No," I answered quickly.

"Why not?"

"Because you wouldn't know how to ask her to leave. And you know you'll have to go home eventually to get something."

I could hear him let out a short breath, relieved. It crossed my mind that he didn't want her to stay at his place as much as I didn't, and that he felt her return was an invasion of our space just as much as I did. And it crossed my mind that he wished she would go away again, so we could continue to work us out.

But the thought didn't stick.

"You don't have to do this," he said softly.

"I know."

"I'm really sorry about our anniversary. I love you."

There was a light tap on my door. "Let's talk about it later," I said before I hung up.

Mali opened my door gently, without waiting for me to grant her permission.

"Thanks," she said.

"Okay" was all I said.

That night I wasn't the only person who couldn't sleep. When I went into the kitchen Mali was already there, smoking a cigarette in her underwear. Her dark hair flowed around her face and she looked peaceful. The same bottle of wine she had earlier was on the table. She poured herself a glass and let it sit. She let the smoke fill the room.

I turned to leave.

"Sit down," she said.

We stared at each other for a long time and when I didn't say anything, she stood up and went to the refrigerator. She opened the door and stared into it. There wasn't a hint of cellulite anywhere on her body. No scars, no nicks, no bruises, no pubic hair. She pulled a bag of baby carrots from the vegetable box, and then she noticed me watching her.

"Do you need something?" she asked.

I shook my head.

She sat at the table again. She frowned at me, bit into one of the carrots and chewed slowly. "We used to be friends," she said and looked at me significantly.

That was true. We used to be friends.

"I'm sorry," she continued. "I'm embarrassed about what happened. I left New York because I couldn't face you and I couldn't face him. I came back because I can't hide forever."

"Yes, you can," I said before I left the room.

I hated faculty meetings. They were the most unpleasant part of being an adjunct professor. To make matters worse, I was the youngest adjunct professor in my department and no one respected me. It seemed, most of the time, like the hostility in the meetings was directed at me. The coffee machine was broken; the old guy who taught History of Cinema looked at me even though I never used the coffee machine. The editing room was left unlocked and an expensive piece of equipment was stolen; Zabrowski looked at me. I didn't even teach editing. It was my least favorite subject and everyone knew it. It couldn't have been the Editing professor, who was always losing his keys.

Most of the time I didn't bother to show up to the meetings, hence the personal phone calls from Zabrowski at home. Meetings were unnecessary and boring, in my opinion. Nothing a memo or voice mail couldn't handle. Professor Jones passed a gallstone. Faculty meeting. Professor Walker's wife had another baby. Faculty meeting. Who cares? But for most of these guys, the department was all they had. The meetings were their idea of a social event.

What pissed me off most about Zabrowski's meetings was they were always scheduled on Friday. I taught one class on Friday. Elements of Screenwriting. From five in the evening to eight. I slept late, dragged myself to class, and spent three hours listening to students discuss scripts that were dead ringers for everything Quentin Tarantino wrote. I would nod and say, "Original! Harrowing! Keep going. Can't wait to see the final product." Fridays were the best days of the week.

On that particular Friday I overslept. When I jumped out of bed I heard Mali in the shower. I scrambled around the apartment like a maniac while I waited for her to finish, trying to find enough magazines to keep me busy during the four hours between the meeting and my class at five. I used to go to the movies, but found that some of my students were doing the same thing. There's nothing more irritating than running into an Introduction to Cinema student in a theater and listening to his take on *Citizen Kane* for twenty minutes before the mindless action movie we spent ten bucks to see begins.

When Mali emerged from the shower, a cloud of steam so thick billowed out into the hall I thought it would set off the smoke alarm. She didn't see me and I watched her as she walked into my parents' bedroom and closed the door.

So, I missed the meeting and caught a cold instead. Mali used all of the hot water and I ended up taking a cold shower. By the time I reached the office I shared with another adjunct professor, I was sneezing and the meeting was over. To make matters worse, I ran into Zabrowski. I groaned inwardly, wanting to avoid a long, drawn-out diatribe about the lack of professionalism in my generation. It really irked me that he just happened to be walking past my office at three in the afternoon on his way home.

"Oh. Beck. There you are. I was just about to slip a memo under your door about the meeting you missed."

Zabrowski was in his sixties. He wore old-fashioned suits and bright bow ties and dyed his hair brown. Without fail, the monthly dye job was awful. I often wondered about his wife, and why she let him leave the house looking the way he did. I imagined it was her revenge on him after learning he'd spent their early years together sleeping with pert, eager students.

"Sorry about that." I sneezed.

"I'm thinking about asking the department to put together a fund for you. The Beck Fund. Eventually it could add up to enough money to buy you an apartment in the city. The commute from Brooklyn proves to be more daunting than you've led me to believe."

"The Brooklyn commute is fine," I mumbled. When I was with him I felt like I was in high school. As a student, not a teacher. A few papers fell from my bag and floated all around the hall as I searched for the key to my office. I cursed under my breath as Zabrowski kept talking. I tuned out his words until he said, "So it wasn't a critical meeting. Just a heads-up. Maybe you should send David a congratulatory note."

That caught my attention. Professor David Sims was the second-youngest professor in the department and the only film professor who smiled at me on occasion. I considered him a friend.

"It's always wonderful to see one of us make it to the big screen," Zabrowski added distractedly, tapping a finger on the wall as I struggled to open my office door. "But now comes the difficult part." He looked up and it seemed his eyes settled on me. "Finding his replacement."

Oh God, I thought. David sold that script he's been trying to sell for years and he's out of here.

Why can't that be me? I asked myself.

Because you never finished one, a tiny voice inside my head answered.

"Looking for a permanent?" I asked.

"Are you interested?"

When I took the job, I thought I'd be out of there after a year. I never thought I'd be a teacher for the rest of my life. The thought of saying yes sent a chill through me. It seemed so . . . permanent.

"When do you need an answer?" I asked.

"Soon, Beck," he said as he walked away. "Soon. Have a nice weekend."

I ate soup for lunch and called my apartment three times to check if Mali was still there. I left messages like "Are you there, Mali? It's me, Casey." I wasn't sure if she was actually there, following my instructions not to listen to my messages or answer my phone, or if she was gone. I called John Paul to find out if she'd been in touch, but I couldn't reach him either.

I barely noticed Josh Persichetti, the fireman in my Contemporary Directors class, standing in the doorway. I would have ignored him, but his careful knock on my door made me jump.

"Sorry," he said and smiled. In plainclothes he looked like a normal guy. A normal, good-looking guy.

"Can I help you?" I asked.

"How are you?" He walked inside.

"Fine. Thanks. A slight cold."

"Are you busy?"

We looked at the phone in my hand. "Sort of. Can I help you?"

"Are you finished for the day? I was wondering if we—"

"I have a class at five," I said abruptly. "Do you have a question? You didn't miss anything yesterday."

"What have you been up to?" he asked.

"Not much. I'm working on something. I'm thinking. I'm . . ." I noticed the cups of coffee in his hands. "I'm drinking coffee."

"I brought you coffee," he said.

"Thanks."

He put the cups on my desk. I stared at them.

"One would have been sufficient."

He blushed. "One is for me."

"Oh."

He picked up the second cup, and then he pulled several packets of sugar from his pocket.

"I wasn't sure how you take it."

"Light, no sugar." I picked up the magazine I was reading and put it on my lap. I stared at it for a minute. "Why am I telling you that? You don't need to know that."

"Some things are just nice to know," he said.

"Trust me, it won't be a bonus question on the final exam."

He dropped his eyes for a moment.

"Well, this is very nice of you," I said awkwardly.

He nodded, and there was this sudden silence that wasn't exactly uncomfortable. I picked up my coffee. He was about to say something when someone knocked on the door. I jumped again and spilled the coffee all over the magazine on my lap.

Josh set his cup calmly on the desk and started to pat my lap with a bunch of napkins. He asked me if any of the coffee had touched my legs. I shook my head no.

"Good," he said like he really meant it. He straightened, and tossed the napkins in the garbage.

The woman in the doorway watched us curiously. I stood up, forgetting about the wet magazine. It fell to the floor with a thud.

"I'm sorry," the woman said. "I can come back."

"It's okay," I assured her. "A version of this happens to me every day."

Josh looked at me, opened his mouth slightly. There was

something in his face that I couldn't read. It made me wonder what he saw when he stared at me like that, so intently. We held each other's gaze for a moment. Then he looked at the woman and she smiled when she recognized him.

"Are we finished, Josh?" I asked, trying to sound professional.

"No," he said. "But I have to go. Take care of that cold."

The woman nodded at him as he left. When she looked at me, I smiled and tried to look welcoming. I wasn't good at it. She stared at me strangely, the stare that young women give you when they want to know if you're a threat. I was glad she couldn't tell.

Six

Johnny had a margarita waiting for me. He said he whipped it up the minute he saw my cab pull up. Johnny was my boyfriend at Bobo's Southern Café and Bar. Actually, he was just the bartender. But any man who can make a margarita as sweet as Johnny's should be someone's man. Unfortunately, he wasn't my type. Muscular. Irish. Forty.

Bobo's did well with creative types and pseudocreative types like me. A bartender like Johnny was perfect for that kind of crowd. He didn't take shit from the creative types who thought they were better than him, and he was sympathetic to people like me. That meant every other drink was free.

Ariadne was already there, sitting in one of the cushiony chairs that were so comfortable they made you feel like you could stay the night if it came down to it. She was draped over a huge book, finishing a margarita. I winked my thanks at Johnny and he told me Ariadne already started a tab.

That was the thing about Bobo's. No matter how pretentious it got I always felt like I was among friends.

I took my jacket off and sat down. "David Sims sold a script to Hollywood and quit yesterday. He's not even finishing the semester."

Ariadne stuck a cigarillo in her mouth and lit it. Of her many talents, the one that impressed me most was her ability to speak with a lit cigarillo in her mouth. "Good for him."

"Yeah. I want to be him."

Ariadne gave me a look that said, *What brought this on?* "You don't write scripts."

"I still want to be him."

"You don't want to be a screenwriter."

I looked dubious. "I do. Actually."

She didn't believe me. "Is that true? Or do you want to be David Sims because David isn't living with Mali?"

I sneezed. "I don't live with Mali."

"I was talking about your situation with Larry this morning. The reason why you let her stay." Larry was Ariadne's therapist of two years. She was always going on and on about him, quoting his words like they were Scripture.

"Oh? And what does Larry say?"

"He's not at liberty to say, really. But he'd like you to come see him. He promises not to charge for the initial visit."

"I don't have health insurance," I reminded her. "I don't need therapy anyway."

"We all need some kind of therapy," she said.

"I don't believe in it."

"Without good reason."

So far, Ariadne had been through four therapists in six years, and each reason she left them was a good enough reason to avoid therapy, in my opinion. Her first two therapists fell in love with her, and the third was actually sleeping with one of his patients. Larry was the fourth.

Therapists have more issues than the rest of us. We go to them but who do they go to when, let's say, they find themselves falling madly in love with a patient? As a teacher, I knew how easy it could be to cross boundaries with students. And teachers hardly discuss the personal stuff therapists and patients discuss. In fact, I would get completely irritated when students came to me for advice. I'd sit and listen to their problems with a blank expression on my face, waiting for the kid to realize that no amount of bonding would improve his grade. Sure, there are professors who eat that shit up, especially when it's coming from a pretty young thing, but not me.

I'd sit in my little office, nod, look sympathetic, and say really stupid things like "Rent your favorite movie and watch it alone. Things will seem much brighter tomorrow." I actually said this, never realizing that some of their favorite movies were *Scarface* and *Natural Born Killers*.

So, I can't help but believe that therapists, like me, are just making their shit up as they go along. The difference is they believe it.

"You need a professional to help you get through the pain," Ariadne insisted.

"Are assassins considered professionals?" I asked.

"I'm serious."

"There is no pain."

"This celibacy thing, that's not pain? Three months without sex and that's not about pain? Let me tell you what I think Larry would say to you. Embrace the pain."

"Would he really say that?" I balked. "Because those sound like the words of a quack to me."

"He would also tell you to embrace your anger."

"I'm not angry. Insecure, maybe, but not angry. I spent a lot of time hating this woman and I'm done hating her."

"Bullshit," Ariadne said matter-of-factly, not even looking at me. "Do you expect anyone to believe that after not having sex for three months with the man you supposedly love, you're done hating the woman who provoked the dry spell in the first place? I bet even John Paul doesn't believe that, and he's not smart."

"Well, I don't hate her."

Ariadne played with the plastic monkey on the rim of her glass. Then she sighed and looked at me.

"This is what I think," she said, taking the cigarillo out of her mouth. "You aren't honest with yourself. You're not happy in this relationship. I think John Paul makes you lonely. Celibacy makes you lonely. And suddenly, the woman he had an affair with knocks on your door and you take her in. *You let her stay overnight.*"

"What was I supposed to do? It was raining."

"A little rain never hurt anybody," Ariadne advised.

"We used to be friends."

"She is *not* a friend anymore."

"She had nowhere to go."

Ariadne rolled her eyes. "I really don't believe she had nowhere else to go. If you did a little digging you would have found that out. But I don't think you wanted to find that out. You want to keep an eye on her. I bet some part of you admires her, wants to be her. Because you think she has it all worked out. You think she can take him away from you and keep him. But that's your mistake. She wouldn't have stepped inside your apartment if she was sure he'd take her back."

"I don't look up to her," I said defensively. "I've looked up to a lot of women, and I've turned to them for help. But not Mali. Never Mali."

Ariadne held up her hands in surrender.

"There were times when I thought everyone I envied or admired could help me get through my problems," I continued. "I thought they could explain *me*. But all of the strong women I admire, you not included, are more fucked up than I am. They aren't better at life, just better at hiding who they really are. I never wanted to be anyone, especially not Mali."

Ariadne tilted her head, unbelieving.

I sighed and added quietly, "Okay. I wanted to be the person she makes people believe she is. That was the person without flaws."

"Even the people we invent have flaws." She stuck the cigarillo back in her mouth and sat forward. "If he kept his dick in his pants, this whole thing never would have happened."

"If she said no once it was out of his pants, this whole thing wouldn't have happened."

Ariadne chuckled. "I'm not defending her, believe me, but you have to punish him before you punish her."

"We haven't had sex in three months."

"That's punishing *you*, sweetheart."

"You're right. Masturbation is definitely not all it's cracked up to be."

"Tell me about it," she said. "I'm getting another drink. You want one?"

We'd barely finished the margaritas in front of us, but the bar was crazy. I could see her point.

"Okay."

A couple of guys stopped her before she reached the bar and tried to make conversation.

Guys were crazy about Ariadne. But it was never in an I-want-to-take-you-home-and-make-love-to-you-all-night kind of way. It was always in an I-*really*-dig-talking-to-you-at-

the-bar-but-if-something-viable-comes-along-well-you-un-
derstand kind of way. Whenever we were at Bobo's, or any
other bar, some guy would inevitably remember her from
some other night and it would be obvious he wanted her to
drop me and help him pass the time talking. Ariadne never
dropped me, but sometimes, when the guy was especially cute,
I could tell she wanted to. I'd say, "Go on. I'm good here on my
own," and she'd say, "Friends last longer."

Ariadne returned with two margaritas.

"To good health and happiness and getting that crazy bitch
out of your house. Mazel tov."

We took long, healthy swallows of our drinks then sat for a
long time, silent.

"Do you really wish you were David Sims?" she asked.

I considered for a minute. "I want to accomplish something."

"Then why not move to California? Your parents would love
that."

"Get the hell out of here."

"You can't accomplish anything in New York. Too much
baggage."

A short guy with steamy glasses and a very thin mustache
stopped at our table. He stared at Ariadne and she stared back.

"Haven't I seen you somewhere before?" he asked after a
minute.

"Yes," she answered coldly. "That's why I don't go there anymore."

The man looked wounded. I felt sorry for him.

"If it wasn't for the mustache and glasses, he would have
been cute," I told her as he disappeared into the crowd.

"And the face, Casey. If it wasn't for the face . . . Are you
ready to go?"

I finished my drink and stood up. I couldn't believe it was almost midnight. As we moved through the crowd toward the exit, I realized I was a little drunk. It didn't take much these days.

I returned home to an empty apartment. All three messages on my answering machine were for Mali. They were from me.

Seven

Saturday was brunch day, one of the rituals John Paul and I had become accustomed to as a couple. Despite my blasé attitude about the whole thing, I loved brunch just as much as the other guy. It was two uninterrupted hours with my boyfriend. No television. No telephone. Just John Paul and me.

We waited twenty minutes without speaking to be seated in a diner called No Place Like Home. Not even the usual "Wow, this place is packed," or "Nice day. Wanna walk in the park after this?" He didn't even ask me how I was feeling, and he knew I was fighting a cold.

John Paul ordered an omelet as soon as we were seated. I ordered blueberry pancakes. He opened the *New York Times* and started reading. I knew what was happening. I was getting John Paul's version of the silent treatment. He was angry because I'd called him early that morning and asked if Mali was with him.

Not only had I called way before he planned to wake up, I'd accused him of harboring an apparent fugitive.

"Why would I let her stay here without telling you?" he asked.

His place was the only place I thought she would go.

"You don't trust me," he said.

When his omelet arrived, he folded the newspaper into a small, anal square and dug in. He didn't even wait for me. In another time, another place, this wouldn't have bothered me. But there, at that moment, under those circumstances, I was incredibly annoyed. I watched him mash his omelet up so that he was actually eating scrambled eggs. He hadn't looked at me once since we'd been seated.

The sight of the yellow disaster on his plate and the sound of shrieking children running around the diner made me sick. It seemed everyone in that diner had a kid, a ring, or the bored, satisfied look of a person who'd done the marriage thing.

And it's not that I wanted to be married. I didn't want children either. I wanted something more. I wanted to feel secure. I wanted to know the man seated across from me was there, not out of habit, but because he really wanted to be. I didn't want to know it because he told me how beautiful I was or how happy he was to be with me. I didn't want him to talk shit to me if he didn't mean it. I wanted to know it because he noticed my pancakes hadn't arrived and he offered to give me his omelet.

Five minutes later the waitress set a plate of blueberry pancakes in front of me and apologized for the delay. John Paul looked up, surprised. He stared at me like it was my fault I hadn't pointed out he was having brunch without me. I started to eat.

"Hey," he said. "I didn't realize . . . "

I could see that he felt badly. He never liked to see me hungry. I concentrated on my pancakes again.

After a minute, he took my chin in his hand and tilted my face upward to look at him. "Are you up for drinking with the crew tonight?" he asked.

I'm up for a drink right now, I wanted to say. "Why wouldn't I be?"

"Because you said you had a hangover."

"No. I said I had a headache. It had nothing to do with drinking last night."

He dropped his fork on his plate, irritated. "What are you pissed off about?"

I looked at him, didn't answer.

He picked up his fork, started eating again.

"We're going to a new place tonight," he said when he finished his omelet. "A few blocks from Maddalena's."

John Paul and Peter never went anywhere other than Maddalena's. I took a wild guess. "Something Mali suggested?"

He nodded. "Yes, actually."

"So, you did speak to her."

"No." He shook his head. "She left a message on the machine yesterday."

Had she called from my apartment before she left, hoping to secure a place on his sofa? And how did she get his number? "Did she say where she's staying?"

He shook his head again. "I didn't know she wasn't staying with you until you called me this morning."

Early in our relationship John Paul and I established Friday nights as the nights we caught up with our separate lives. I always met Ariadne at Bobo's. John Paul had drinks with his coworkers or Peter at Maddalena's. It was the same old thing all the time. I never had any reason to wonder where he'd been. I thought I knew.

"What did you end up doing last night?" I asked.

"I stayed in," he said, surprised. "Why?"

"I called you around nine and you weren't there."

He narrowed his eyes. "Are you sure you called *me?*"

Well, I hadn't actually called him. "Maybe I dialed a wrong number," I said.

He sighed. It was the sigh that said, *You don't trust me.*

"Why don't you invite Ariadne tonight?" he asked.

John Paul hated Ariadne, and that was his way of waving a white flag. I think she scared him. Often, she would just stare at him dully while he spoke, never making an effort to comment on anything he said. Ariadne had a knack for making people feel uncomfortable, but I suspected she enjoyed John Paul's uneasiness in particular.

I didn't answer him.

He flagged the waitress down and asked for the check before I finished my pancakes.

I had to give Mali credit. Portal was a very interesting choice. Ariadne warned me it was a college bar and popular with working-class kids, kids from our school. When I asked her to meet us she said she wouldn't be caught dead there. And she wasn't in the mood to spend her Saturday night with Mali and John Paul.

I arrived after eleven. I knew I had the right place when I spotted men in the worn jeans and flannel shirts that scream Bridge-and-Tunnel-goes-to-City-University-of-New-York crowded around the entrance with giant mugs of beer in their hands. I thought I recognized one of them.

I felt their eyes go over me as I struggled with the heavy iron door, from which the name Portal was derived, I assumed. Finally, one of them grabbed the door for me and I thanked him. Whoever said chivalry was dead was wrong.

Portal was packed to capacity, which explained all of the men braving the cold outside. For a minute I regretted arriving so late. I hated muscling my way into packed bars and having beer spilled all over me before the evening began.

As I walked to the bar, I crunched. I thought it was my shoes, but when I looked down I realized peanut shells were covering the floor like a carpet. And as I looked up I saw everyone around me cracking open peanuts and spitting the shells on the floor. I imagined John Paul and Peter standing off in a corner somewhere, looking completely wooden in their expensive clothes, dodging peanut shells like two wimps in a batting cage.

I ordered a shot of Cuervo and sucked it down on the spot. It helped a little. I felt ready to brave the mass of eyes creeping all over my body like I was fresh meat.

"Thank God you're here." Gabriella grabbed my arm and pulled me close to her before I could order a second drink. The eyes of several flanneled men watched us curiously. "I just had to fight off a pack of twenty-year-olds coming out of the bathroom. What kind of place is this?"

As usual, Gabriella looked very pretty. She was wearing black velvet pants that showed off just how thin and worked out she was, and a glittery silver shirt only she could get away with. Her face was lightly made up so that her very big green eyes stood out under bangs of thick, blond hair.

"God, it's so glaringly loud in here," she complained, lighting a cigarette.

"Well, it is a bar," I said, though it did seem louder than most bars we went to.

"I'm getting old." She sucked on her cigarette. "Why are you so late? John Paul's having a fit. Probably thinks you ran off with one of these boys. Though I wouldn't blame you if you had. Some of them are very attractive."

Yes. She was right about that. The men may have been young, but they were cute. They had that rugged irresistibility about them that commercials are always using to sell products. You could just smell the Old Spice and Budweiser beer.

"Let's get you a drink," she said.

She turned back to the bar and flagged down the bartender, a Mohawked man with tattoos all over his body. I thought Mohawks went out in the eighties. Gabriella ordered two complicated drinks consisting of vodka, blue curaçao, gin and a drop of vermouth. She instructed him officiously on how to make the drinks just right, despite his seasoned indifference.

"I've got the first round." She handed me the very blue drink.

"Is Dock here?" I asked, sipping it cautiously. It wasn't half bad.

"He was here. But Polo wanted to leave. He asked me to tell you he'd give you a call." She shrugged. "He's such a sweet guy. I can't figure out what he sees in her. She's that perfect kind of suspicious that makes a man tired very fast."

"Yeah, well," I said, not wanting to dive right into that conversation.

"And Mali looks good," she added. "She's got that Spanish-Puerto-Rican-Latina thing going on."

"I think she is Puerto Rican," I said.

"Who knows. I met her grandmother years ago. She was white. Like, white-hair-blue-eyes white. I think she's biracial. But I'm still reeling from the fact that she showed up at your apartment the other night."

"So am I."

"Oh, and sorry I didn't call her. It got crazy at work."

I shrugged. "She isn't staying with me anymore."

"She told me. She takes off and now she reappears being very cryptic about where she stayed last night. John Paul's been trying to get it out of her." She rolled her eyes. "Not that it's any of my business, but *I'm dying to know.*"

While I wasn't dying to know, I was curious. What was the big secret? Mali had always been something of a nomad in the old days, sleeping on John Paul and Peter's sofa when she had nowhere else to go....

"As long as she didn't stay with John Paul and Peter," I said.

Gabriella shrugged, sipped her drink. "You see them yet?"

I assumed she meant John Paul and Mali, and by the tone of her voice I imagined they were probably too close for comfort.

"Where is he?" I asked.

"Standing around," Gabriella said vaguely. "Don't worry. He doesn't seem very happy with her. He's actually kind of angry and abrupt. That's a good sign, isn't it?"

I scanned the bar for a glimpse of him. I wasn't sure if it was a good sign or not. Anger meant he felt something.

"Don't look now," Gabriella warned. "But a very delicious person is staring at you."

Of course I looked. The problem with starting a statement with the words *Don't look now* is that the person you say them to will definitely look before you explain why she shouldn't.

And there was Josh Persichetti. He was standing at the other end of the bar looking very comfortable in the Bridge-and-Tunnel crowd, and very "delicious" in a tight, red sweater. He stared at me boldly, unfazed by the fact that I was staring back. Immediately I understood why Ariadne wouldn't be caught dead here. Conflict of interest.

He raised his bottle of Budweiser like he was making a toast.

I did the same with my blue drink just as a pretty young thing leaned over and whispered something in his ear.

"Who is that?" Gabriella sounded awed, which surprised me. She always tried to keep a certain level of indifference when it came to men.

"Don't get crazy. He's a student."

"You're fucking a student and you didn't tell me?" she nearly screamed.

"Calm down," I hissed. "I am not fucking a student."

"Well, you should be. I had my eye on him the minute he walked in." She winked at me.

"You would cheat on Peter?"

She looked defensive. "No. But I'm not dead. I can still talk shit."

I stared at her a little longer and she stared at the floor. Then she sighed. I knew what she was thinking. It would be nice, kind of, to be out there again.

"He's a fireman," I said.

"That explains it."

I started to feel dizzy. I took another gulp from my drink, which was deceptively strong. Some people started to move past me, and I saw John Paul and Mali and Peter across the bar. Mali was blabbing, and John Paul and Peter were totally engrossed in whatever she was saying.

"Casey?"

I jumped. It was Josh. He pointed at my drink. "That looks bad."

"It isn't."

"Yeah, but will you remember *anything* in the morning?"

"Great point," I said, remembering the shot of tequila I had when I first arrived. "I should stick to beer." I put the blue drink on the bar and turned back to him.

"How are you?" he asked.

"Good. You?"

"Great," he said.

Gabriella watched him, acknowledging his beauty. He felt her eyes on him and turned to look at her.

"Josh." He held out his hand.

Gabriella sparkled flirtatiously as she took it. I felt jealous for a millisecond as I saw Josh notice her slowly, the way any normal man in the world would. His eyes went over her body casually and she struck a subtle pose, making it easier for him.

"Nice to meet you," he said and turned back to me. "How are you?" he asked again.

"Still doing okay over here," I said.

Gabriella faded away behind him. She stood at the bar, keeping an ear open for anything he might say. She wanted to be able to discuss him with me later. I took comfort in her being there, like a guardian angel.

"You want another drink?" he asked into my ear so he wouldn't have to shout.

"No. I'm good, thanks."

"You look good."

"Thanks." I smiled.

"It's nice to see you this way."

"What way?"

He grinned. "Standing here, hanging, drinking."

I looked at the bar for something to hold on to.

"So, do you have brothers and sisters?" he asked out of the blue.

"I'm a single child," I shouted before I realized what I said. "Only child, excuse me."

"I like single." He laughed. "I have an older brother and sister."

"Oh." I nodded. "The youngest. Your mom must be protective."

"Yeah. Sister, too."

I nodded, imagining that meeting. We stood without speaking for a while, and then I saw his hand reach out for me. I wasn't ready for contact so I turned to the bar and gulped a shot of tequila that was just sitting there.

"You just . . . never mind. I'll get it." He took a crumpled five from his pocket and paid for the tequila shot I consumed mistakenly. He looked at me, stepped closer and put his mouth to my ear again.

"You don't have to fight it," he said.

"Fight what?"

"We're obviously attracted to each other," he answered softly, carefully. He pulled back to see my face. I hoped it was expressionless. He smirked, which led me to believe it wasn't, and came back to my ear. "It's okay."

Holy shit, I was thinking. I could feel something happening in my face that hadn't happened in a long time with anyone except John Paul. I was blushing.

"Aren't you here with someone?" I asked, trying to change the subject but failing.

He grinned. I supposed he thought the question opened a door to my true, inner feelings.

"I'm with some buddies from work. And their wives. You wanna meet them?"

"No," I answered too quickly. "Thanks."

"Do you mind if I ask how old you are?"

Instinctively I looked at Gabriella, who was indeed looking at me. She nodded her head in the affirmative and I said, "Twenty-nine. You?"

Gabriella shook her head to indicate *wrong question, bad move.*

"Twenty-three," he said.

"Oh."

"Do you like motorcycles?" he asked.

"Why?"

"I'd like to give you a ride home on my bike," he told me.

"I just got here."

"When we're ready to go."

"You want to take me to Brooklyn on the back of a motorcycle?" I asked.

"I live in Brooklyn. I ride out there all the time."

"There's a reason why they call you New York's Bravest."

"Don't say no."

He reached out to touch me and just as I decided I wanted to be touched by him, he stopped. Someone behind me wrapped his arms around my neck.

"Welcome to working-class hell," Peter said, planting a kiss on my cheek. He stared at Josh for a minute and Josh shifted uncomfortably. Then Peter held out his right hand for Josh to shake and kept his left arm wrapped around my neck. "Nice to meet you. I'm Peter."

"Josh," Josh said.

"What the hell kind of place is this?" Peter asked. "That Mali is a card."

He let go of me, biting my earlobe playfully before going to Gabriella and planting kisses on her neck. Josh watched them flirt. I could tell he was noticing what a supercouple they were. Pretty and blond and all-American. When he looked at me again his eyes were questioning. *Who is this guy in the snakeskin boots, and why are all the girls letting him suck on their faces?*

I was going to explain that Peter and Gabriella were my friends and it was okay; Peter kissed everyone. For some reason, Gabriella didn't mind. But I saw Mali heading in our direction. And there was John Paul walking over slowly, behind her, eyes focused on me, looking heart-stoppingly handsome as usual. He stood next to Josh, glanced at him, nodded. He looked at me again and smiled and his smile said, *I've had a few drinks and . . . can we be friends again?*

Mali noticed and leaned into me. She said, "We've been looking for you."

I pulled away from her and looked at John Paul. I tried to discern whether or not they'd been fighting, but they would not look at each other and I wasn't sure. Josh looked confused as Mali introduced herself and asked why they had never met before. He glanced at me.

Mali said, "You do know each other, don't you? You weren't trying to pick our little Casey up, were you?"

"No," I said, wanting to strangle her. There I was, trying to establish this age boundary between Josh and me, and Mali ruined it by making me look like a child. "Josh is one of my students."

"Oh," Mali said. "That's sweet."

Josh looked embarrassed and I regretted saying it. And Mali smiled at me like I was just the cutest little thing she ever did see. I wanted to kill her, but I didn't think I had the energy.

"We love Casey. Casey is wonderful," Mali announced out of the blue. Josh lost his self-consciousness and beamed. Mali smiled at the look on his face. He had reacted exactly the way she expected him to.

"She's a great professor." He smiled at me. "A great person."

John Paul looked at Josh again. A little more closely. A little longer. He looked at Josh's clothes, shoes, face. And then he looked at me, curious.

"Yes. Casey's a good woman," Mali agreed, glancing at John Paul. "I found myself stranded in Brooklyn the other night and Casey let me stay with her. Despite our rocky past."

"Oh." Josh nodded and looked at my friends. He realized they were sizing him up and he blushed.

"Where are you staying now?" I asked Mali. All eyes turned away from Josh and settled on her. It was the question of the hour.

Mali sighed melodramatically, tilted her head to one side and opened her eyes real wide so that she looked like a very appetizing damsel in distress.

"Well, here's the unfortunate deal," she began, looking at all of us, making sure we were listening. "I gave up my apartment before I went away. I was in touch with a former classmate and I was supposed to be moving in with her for a while, but I think we got the dates mixed up. She's out of town. So, basically, I'm screwed. I don't even have a job lined up."

John Paul and Peter stared at the floor and Gabriella looked far off at a wall or something. Josh was the only one who seemed concerned.

"Family?" he asked.

Mali shook her head. "Not an option."

Josh looked at me and I raised my eyebrows like there was nothing left to say. He frowned slightly. I realized he just thought I was mean.

"Well," I stuttered. I didn't know why I cared what he thought of me. "You know, my parents' bedroom is still empty."

Everyone looked at me sharply and I wanted to take the

words from her ears and swallow them again. But I couldn't. They were out there. And Mali was actually considering.

"You can have the sofa," Peter offered and Gabriella hit his arm. "Or not," he added quickly. "I mean, a bed sounds like a better deal."

Mali looked at John Paul and he looked at her. She wanted him to ask her. For a moment the rest of us weren't there. It wasn't lost on me how right they looked. They shared the same space. He didn't have to look down to look at her.

"You can stay with me," Gabriella said firmly as if to say, *We're all adults and we know why Mali can't stay with anyone else.* "Just bring your stuff over later. I'll leave a key under the doormat."

I could tell Mali was disappointed. Gabriella leaned against the bar and Josh watched as Peter wiped something off her shirt and kissed her. He watched Mali turn her attention back to him and sigh, bored.

"We should exchange numbers," she told him. "There's always some dinner party or movie night happening at someone's apartment. We're all close friends. We have a history together. You should come. Be a part of it."

Josh took a swig from his Bud, his eyes on me. "Casey has my number."

Mali looked at me as well, smirked. "And I've got Casey's number."

I looked at John Paul and he was staring at me, eyes narrowed.

"Just one of the perks of the job, huh?" Mali asked, nodding her head toward Josh.

"You bet." I was being sarcastic.

Mali laughed. "How do you teach under so much pressure? How do you resist temptation?"

I shrugged.

"Are we as celibate as we say we are?" Mali asked.

"Of course," Gabriella said, mainly to John Paul, before I could say anything.

John Paul's eyes slid away from me to see Gabriella. His face relaxed. And then he held out his hand to Josh. "Nice to meet you, buddy," he said, as though it was Josh's cue to leave.

Josh stared at the hand. The cue wasn't lost on him, but he wasn't sure if he wanted to obey it. He looked confused, and he was fighting a blush. He had found things out about me he hadn't expected, I assumed. He didn't know what to do with the information.

John Paul put a hand on my elbow and asked if I was ready to leave. Josh looked at me strangely. It hadn't dawned on him that I was actually with someone. I tried not to read into the fact that he assumed I wasn't. He looked around for his friends, and then he looked at me fleetingly as he turned to leave, saying something like "See you in school."

I pretended not to watch him walk away.

Eight

So he's a fireman," Gabriella said, placing a large bowl of salad greens in the middle of the table. We were having a late lunch at her apartment. Gabriella rarely invited me to her apartment, and she never offered to cook. But her introduction to Josh the night before led her to believe my life was much more exciting than she had thought, and the fact that Mali was staying with her made her invitation for lunch more appetizing to me. "Don't get me wrong. I love John Paul. *Adore him.* But there's nothing like a secret admirer. Even though this guy isn't exactly secret. He had radar from, like, across the room."

"Yeah." I nodded as she went back into the kitchen for the rest of the meal. "I-want-a-better-grade radar."

"That's so not true," she shot back. "If he wanted a better grade, he would have left with any one of the beautiful girls trying to get his attention once he realized you were with John

Paul. But he only had eyes for the one truly beautiful *woman* in there."

I laughed.

"Believe me," Gabriella continued, carrying a bowl of tuna fish salad out of the kitchen. She hadn't cooked after all. "He looked truly disappointed. Guys can't make that shit up at the spur of the moment. He wasn't expecting a John Paul, and then he got one and he was upset. He was like, how do I compete with a stunning black man like that?"

I nearly choked up my tomato juice.

"It's true," she insisted, sitting down across from me. "Did John Paul say anything about it when you got home?"

"No." As usual, John Paul and I had gone back to my place and watched television before we fell asleep.

"I could tell he sensed something," Gabriella said. "The way he looked at Josh. He was jealous. That's a good sign."

I didn't know what kind of sign it was.

"I'm afraid of guys like Josh," I admitted. "He just shows up and is suddenly enamored with me. What's that about?"

"It's about you being cute and having great tits." She scooped some of the tuna onto her plate. "Young guys love that shit."

"Right."

"It's true."

"He seems too good," I said. "He's cute and sweet and definitely not the kind of guy who just likes breasts."

"How do you know?"

"He brought me coffee. No one ever brings me coffee to the office. Not even Ariadne."

"Ariadne doesn't want to sleep with you."

"This guy doesn't want to sleep with me."

Gabriella gave me that look that said, *Who are you kidding?*

"You don't pay for some chick's tequila shot when it's not even hers. You take off when she drinks someone else's drink."

I flushed as I remembered that unfortunate moment. "Well, I can't help thinking a guy like Josh is bound to get really fat and bitter, and bellow for dinner and a beer while he's watching football," I said.

"Or he could get killed fighting a fire," she said. "You're not marrying him. You're not even looking for a date. You're in a very serious, very stable relationship with a wonderful man. But why not enjoy this? There's no crime in enjoying it."

"Wonderful in what way?" I asked.

Gabriella picked up a lettuce leaf and smeared tuna on it. "What?"

People were always saying John Paul was wonderful, and they were always admiring how stable we were, and I wondered what they saw when they saw us. I hated when people said he was wonderful. Part of me was jealous and annoyed that he hadn't saved that part of himself for me alone. I was just like everyone else in his life. Only I saw the flaws as well. And I wanted to tell the people who called him wonderful and stable that they should really get to know him, to start fucking him. Then we'd discuss how wonderful and stable he was.

"Wonderful in what way?" I repeated. "Specifically."

Gabriella looked at me like I was crazy. She shrugged. "I don't know. Why? What's wrong with you?"

Gabriella wasn't the type of girl you had meaningful conversations with. You couldn't ask her to get into specifics. I grabbed a couple of slices of bread and made myself a sandwich. "Forget it," I said.

She smiled absently.

"By the way, thanks for letting Mali stay here," I said.

Gabriella stuffed tuna into her mouth. "I'm not doing it for you. It was just a really stupid moment and I'm the only one who doesn't have an issue with her, you know?"

I nodded.

"And I didn't want her staying in the same apartment as my boyfriend either . . . Speak of the devil." We heard the sound of a key in the lock. "She said she'd be out most of the day."

Mali walked into the apartment carrying a paper bag. She stopped short when she saw me.

"Well, well, well," she said. "This is where the girls come to nurse their hangovers."

"I live here," Gabriella reminded her.

"I bought tacos." Mali held up the bag. "The only true way to avoid a hangover is avoid drinking altogether. Or drink loads of water before you go to bed. I know people who take aspirins. But I'd be afraid of liver damage. Tomato juice is also supposed to do the trick, but I like to think eating and sleeping are the best medicine." She looked at my bulging sandwich. "I see you do, too."

Gabriella laughed uncomfortably.

"You aren't sore about last night, are you?" Mali asked me.

"Why would I be sore about last night?"

"Well, I hope you didn't get too bent out of shape when I exchanged numbers with your student."

"No problem," I said casually. I didn't know she had succeeded in getting Josh's number. But John Paul and I did leave Portal before everyone else.

"You sure? You looked horrified when I asked for it the first time."

"You imagined that," I said.

Gabriella stood up and pointed to the bag. "What'd you get?"

"Tacos," Mali said. "Real ones. With black beans and cheese and *pollo*. There's enough for you, Casey. Do you want one?"

"No. Thanks," I said.

"Me, neither." Gabriella rubbed her stomach. "We had tuna."

Mali made a face and carried the bag into the kitchen. Gabriella mouthed the word *Sorry.* A couple of minutes later, Mali came back into the room, biting into a taco and asking if we were finished with the tuna.

"I hate the smell," she said, her mouth full of black beans and cheese and *pollo.* "It sticks with you all day."

I imagined all the days I'd spent smelling like tuna without even realizing it.

"How was London?" Gabriella asked, removing the bowl of tuna from the table and carrying it into the kitchen.

"London," I said. "Is that where you've been?"

Mali nodded.

"What happened to your sense of adventure? Why not Chechnya?"

"Ha, ha," Mali said dryly. "To answer your question, Gabriella, it's the most beautiful city I've ever seen. Have you ever been there?"

Gabriella came back into the room, cleaning her hands with a wet paper towel. "I've been to England but not London. Isn't that weird?"

"It's like no other place in the world," Mali told us. "Where else can you look out of a window and see so much history?"

"Birmingham, Appomattox, Chicago," I said.

Mali rolled her eyes. "You know what I mean."

"Did you make a lot of friends?" Gabriella asked.

Mali perked up. As she talked nonstop about her flat and her flatmates, Gabriella brought out a bottle of wine. The best way to avoid a hangover is to keep drinking.

"How's school?" Mali asked me.

I shrugged. "Good."

"What's it like? Do you teach that *Birth of a Nation* bull-shit?"

I shook my head, too embarrassed to admit that I did. I was required to. But I was hardly enthusiastic about it. We rarely spent more than two class hours on the 1915 film when I taught Introduction to Cinema. And even then, I always made sure to point out no student needed to view it for any other reason except a better grade on an exam.

"I hated that shit," she said.

"You studied film?" Gabriella was suddenly fascinated. So was I. As long as I'd known Mali, I'd never known she studied film. I stared at her and wondered if we would have been friends if not for John Paul.

"Film originally was my major in college." She shrugged. "Couldn't hack it . . . all of those egotistical . . . " She stopped, looked at me.

"I feel the same way about dance," I said.

"I never understood why teachers felt the need to screen *Birth of a Nation* and *Triumph of the Will* every five minutes," she went on. "Then there'd be these students who'd spit that artistic-license crap in your face when you reminded them Leni Riefenstahl was a Nazi and Griffith was a racist. You know what I mean, right?"

There were always a few kids who claimed they loved *Birth of a Nation* and *Triumph of the Will.* That always killed me. I put them up there with the kids who said *Citizen Kane* was their all-time-favorite movie. There was one black woman who spent ten minutes of class time telling me how magnifi-cent the close-ups in *Birth of a Nation* were. Too bad she was a great student. I wanted to fail her for being such a kiss-ass.

"I'll never understand artists," Mali said.

"You're an artist," I pointed out.

"I'm a dancer. There's a difference."

"Is there? I bet you don't say that when you're trying to get a grant."

She didn't look like she understood what I meant. "What kind of scripts do you inspire your students to write?" she asked.

"Inspire?" I laughed. "I don't inspire my students to do anything."

Mali looked at Gabriella. "To hear Josh tell it—"

"Maybe I inspire them to write the next *Long Kiss Goodnight*," I cut her off. "I like action."

"*Long Kiss Goodnight*, Casey? Come on," Mali moaned. "That isn't very responsible of you."

"I don't take responsibility for anything my students do," I told her.

"So you don't care if they turn out *shit* that makes them millions and corrupts people's minds?"

"Millions," Gabriella said. "Doesn't sound bad to me. And wouldn't a movie that made millions give them a chance to make anything they wanted afterward?"

"Yes," I said, even though I knew that wasn't always true.

Mali made a face and disappeared inside the kitchen.

"Why don't we ditch her and go out for a while?" Gabriella suggested quietly.

I declined. "I have to read fifteen scripts for class. I've been holding on to them forever."

Gabriella looked depressed.

"What? What did I say?"

She shook her head. "It's stupid, really. It's just . . . you're so together. You have a great career and a great man. You've got students worshiping the ground you walk on. And you're being

completely strong and grounded about the whole Mali thing.
If I were in your place I'd be popping Valium or something. I
wish . . . " She shook her head. "Forget it. It's stupid."

"It's forgotten." I smiled uncomfortably. It's weird how people perceive things so differently from how they really are.

The doorbell rang. Gabriella stood up to answer it. Mali
came out of the kitchen to see who it was.

Peter and John Paul walked in. I stood up, surprised to see
them. John Paul was carrying a bottle of Wild Turkey. Peter
was carrying a grocery bag.

"Hey," John Paul greeted Gabriella, pecking her cheek and
putting the bottle on the table. He took off his coat and flung it
on a chair. Peter did the same thing. They didn't notice me.

"You're kidding." Mali grinned at the bottle.

"We bought sour mix just in case," John Paul said.

"Too bad I hate whiskey," I said.

John Paul and Peter turned around to see me.

"Casey." John Paul gave me a warm hug without missing a
beat. "You said you were going to school this morning."

"Mmmm, I did, didn't I?" I moved away from him. "What
are you doing here?"

"We came to celebrate," Peter answered for him.

"Celebrate?" I asked.

John Paul nodded. "Gabriella got Mali a job at the café."

"You did?" I looked at Gabriella. We had spent the afternoon together and she failed to mention it. That she had become the Helpful Friend.

"I didn't really get her a job." Gabriella tried to sound light.
"It was a strange coincidence. Mali answered the phone this
morning when my boss called. He told her that he was looking
for another waitress."

"Wow. How lucky can you get?" I turned my attention back to John Paul. "And Mali called you at my place? And you brought whiskey?"

"I called him," Peter said. "Don't burst an ovary, Casey. You weren't home. We thought you were working."

"I didn't want to disturb you," John Paul added.

I sat down again and took the advice I thought Larry would give me if I could afford to be his patient: relax and embrace the humiliation.

John Paul sat next to me. He put his arm around my shoulder and kept his eyes on me. I sensed he wanted to look at *her*, wanted to figure out what was different about her, but he was avoiding her for my benefit.

Like most people who have been away for a long time, Mali looked refreshed and healthy. A woman who had experienced things we hadn't. She was older, somehow. She said things like "You never know how much you love a place until you leave it," and she talked about hitchhiking to Germany and driving a hundred miles an hour on the Autobahn. She smoked "first-rate" hash in coffee shops in Amsterdam and ate smoked herring in Denmark on the street.

John Paul loved people's stories and I didn't want to take away his right to be fascinated by Mali's tales. I wanted to take away her right to tell them.

"I sent the fish back because it was too salty," Mali was saying. "When the waitress came out of the kitchen, Ray asked if he could talk to her for a second. So, here's this guy I just spent the night with, this guy who claimed he wasn't hungry and never ate lunch, whispering in our waitress's ear. And I'm sitting there, wondering what the hell is going on. After a minute, the waitress pulled away, like he bit her or something, and said the fish was probably in the garbage."

John Paul and Peter started to laugh, anticipating the rest of the story. I wasn't in the mood. It was a shame, because I love a funny story. And I loved laughing with John Paul. He had a deep, mischievous laugh that I adored. But I felt like I was no longer a part of the equation. I felt like I was sitting with the wrong group of friends.

"Imagine how *I* felt," Mali continued, enjoying the attention. "I was sitting there, horrified, praying he hadn't asked what I thought he asked. I already felt bad for sending the food back."

John Paul laughed harder. Mali started to laugh, too.

"So, the waitress came out of the kitchen again with a take-out bag. She handed it to Ray and he asked, all deadpan and shit, whether or not she'd be angry if he ate it in the restaurant."

John Paul let out a howl. Peter banged his hands on the table and stomped his feet. I looked at Gabriella. The expression on her face was unreadable. I wasn't sure about her, but I certainly didn't get it.

When Mali offered John Paul and Peter tacos, they accepted. Mali ate with them.

"Eating chicken these days?" Peter asked her.

John Paul glanced at her, then at me.

"I've always eaten chicken," she answered without looking at Peter.

"No," he challenged. "You were a vegan."

"Funny, I don't remember," she said brusquely.

Peter stared at her a minute longer, shook his head, and chuckled. John Paul stared at the table. There was a look of intense concentration on his face. Peter was right. Mali used to be a vegan and John Paul was trying to remember that. Why did I?

"Where did you stay Friday night?" Gabriella asked Mali.

Mali took a deep breath. "This is going to shock you," she said.

I wondered when she would get tired of starting every story with the refrain "This is going to shock you" to guarantee attention.

"What?" Gabriella said.

"I stayed with my mother."

I had to admit that was pretty good. Her news. It did shock me. Because Mali had always been . . . motherless. But John Paul and Peter didn't seem so impressed. Peter moved to the couch, lay down, and closed his eyes.

"How is she?" John Paul asked.

"Pregnant." Mali pulled a cigarette from a pack in her pocket and lit it. "She is pregnant and obtrusive and I hate her."

"Your mother?" Gabriella wanted to know.

Mali noticed the look on Gabriella's face: a mixture of disbelief and discomfort. She smiled. "I never liked her. Ask John Paul."

We looked at John Paul. The expression on his face warned that this was a subject we needed to stay clear of. A subject not to be messed with.

"This pregnancy thing just compounds the issue," Mali continued.

"You never mentioned a mother," I said.

"Everyone has a mother," she answered curtly.

"Yes," I said. "I know. You never mentioned yours." Actually, I thought she had been hatched from an egg, a reptilian sort of thing.

"John Paul knows her."

I looked at John Paul again. He was trying not to stare at her. I wanted to draw his attention away from her, but I couldn't think of a way to do it. Not with the mother thing hanging out there. Me not wanting him to look at her had nothing to do with me not wanting him to see her. It was more about me not wanting her to think she was worth seeing.

"Shit," Mali said. "Now that I've said it, it doesn't feel like it had to be said." She looked at John Paul significantly. Their eyes met for a minute, and then he looked down, rubbed my leg.

I started to get a headache. When I stood up, he asked where I was going.

"I'm going to help Gabriella clean up, and then I'm going to go home."

John Paul stood up as well. "I'll help you."

I shook my head. "You go. I'll take a cab home."

"No, honey . . . "

"I don't want you to stay," I said abruptly. "And since when do you call me *honey?*"

John Paul frowned at me. "Since all the time, I think," he said.

That wasn't true. He never called me *honey.* And it sounded false. I despised it.

Mali stared at us innocently, as though she weren't the problem. Gabriella motioned for her to help bring the dishes and glasses into the kitchen.

Without a fight, John Paul reached for his jacket. "Call me later," he said.

I nodded, stepping back when he tried to kiss me good-bye.

Mali came out of the kitchen and waved when John Paul left. She sat at the table and lit another cigarette. Our eyes met.

"I'm sorry I threaten you," she said.

"Fuck you."

"It's over." She tried not to smile. "I'm not going to lie to you, Casey. My feelings for John Paul haven't disappeared. In fact, they're very much the same. But we're just friends now.

We have too much history not to be friends. If you can't handle that, fine. Just don't expect me to be a part of it."

I picked up the Wild Turkey bottle John Paul had brought over for her and thought about throwing it. Mali didn't move. She knew I wasn't going to hit her.

Gabriella came out of the kitchen to referee, but I grabbed my coat and left.

I considered avoiding the Polka Dot Puppy coffee shop until the semester ended. But the Polka Dot served great coffee and I was determined not to sacrifice great coffee because my students were keeping tabs on me.

"Have a good day, Ms. Beck," Saul, the counter guy, said. I backed up, surprised. I had no idea who he was. I knew his name was Saul because of his name tag, but it made no sense that he knew mine. I wasn't wearing one.

"Is there a sign on me that I'm unaware of?" I asked.

"What?" He looked baffled.

"Never mind." I turned around and walked into the person behind me. The sip top on my container fell off and coffee spilled on the floor, just missing his feet.

"Is this your thing? Spilling coffee?" I looked up to see Josh. "I'll remember that."

"I'm sorry."

"No problem," he said. "I'm used to hotter things than that."

"Listen, I'm sorry about . . . "

He shook his head. "Let's forget it."

He turned away from me. I stood there for a minute, trying to figure out if I should wait for him and say something else or just leave. He turned slightly but didn't look at me. I assumed it was his way of saying he preferred that I go.

When he sat down in my class twenty minutes after our chance meeting at the Polka Dot Puppy, I knew I wouldn't be able to ignore him. I spent the entire ninety minutes trying not to look at him. From the corner of my eye I could see him doodling in his notebook, raking his hands through his hair, leaning over to listen to something the woman next to him was saying.

It wasn't fair. I knew that I couldn't take a student crush seriously. Because teachers are, no doubt, lonelier and more susceptible than students are. But no student crush in the history of student crushes, I was sure, had ever looked like Josh. And I'd never felt so vulnerable.

The woman in the front row was gabbing about why Hal Hartley's *Trust,* my personal favorite, was an inferior film compared with *Henry Fool,* and how important it is to give filmmakers credit for growing up. I nodded and raised my eyebrows and tried hard to look interested, but I'd never seen *Henry Fool* and I couldn't stop thinking about the fact that Josh and the woman next to him were still whispering in each other's ears. In any other class, with any other students, I would have asked them to shut up.

"I won't be here on Thursday," Josh told me when class was over.

I didn't look up from my notes. "Okay."

"I'll see you," he said.

I looked up this time and smiled. "See you."

The woman he was talking to throughout class was waiting for him by the door. She was casually leaning against the door frame and she smiled seductively when he touched her arm. She said something and he laughed and they disappeared down the hall to their next class.

Nine

I was lounging in bed Monday evening, eating popcorn and channel surfing, when I heard the keys in the door. I listened to John Paul put his briefcase down and take off his coat. He came into the bedroom and found me, already dressed in my pajamas, lying there, staring up at him.

He loosened his tie and slipped out of his shoes. He climbed into the bed with me, lay on his side and watched me for a minute.

"How are you feeling today?" he asked.

I stared at the ceiling. "Good. You? How was work?"

"Shitty day." He turned over on his back, rubbed his eyes and yawned.

"Why?"

"These assholes in the office," he said, sighing deeply, stretching his arms up as though he were trying to touch the ceiling. "Some kid comes in and throws peanut butter on the wall and it's genius. Meanwhile, I torment myself for two weeks to come up with a decent idea for the peanut guys and they ask if I had help. What do I look like?"

I didn't answer.

"I told you about that kid, right? The one with the . . . " He waved his fingers in front of his eyes. "With the twitch."

I still didn't answer. He put his hand on my stomach, under my top. He traced invisible circles on my skin.

"I'm sorry about yesterday," he said. "I wasn't trying to disrespect you by being there."

I sat up, accidentally knocking the bowl of popcorn to the floor. "You slept with this woman," I reminded him. "And she's everywhere."

"I can't stop her from going places."

"I know, but you brought her Wild Turkey and sour mix and I know Wild Turkey is her drink. What if I hadn't been there?"

He covered his face with his hands, frustrated and annoyed with me. "I do not want her," he said slowly. "If I wanted her I would not be with you."

"Don't talk to me like I have a learning disability."

He pressed his hands to his face harder, and then he sat up and slid off the bed. He went into the kitchen and I could hear him banging the refrigerator door open, searching for something to eat. I started to clean up the popcorn from the floor. When he came back into the bedroom he had a beer, and I was holding the bowl of popcorn.

"You want to go away?" he asked. "What do you think of Belgium?"

"I haven't thought of Belgium. Ever."

"We could go to Belgium or Holland or Luxembourg."

"I don't fly," I said.

"I know. But I think we'd be good on a trip like that. I think we'd travel well together."

I thought we'd travel well together, too. But I was thinking more along the lines of a road trip to Massachusetts or Maine.

"How would we get there?" I asked. "To Belgium."

He stared at me for a long time, anger dissipating. He said, "I'll hold your hand the whole time."

I turned away because I didn't want him to see me smile. That was sweet.

"Belgium wouldn't be my first choice," I admitted.

"Okay. What about London?"

"London?" Everywhere we went Mali was there. "You want to go to London like Mali?"

"Oh God," he growled. "Are you going to associate everything I say with Mali? I don't want to be accused. I don't need that here. I get it at work."

I looked down at my hands.

"I'll make you a deal," he said softly. "I'll make dinner at my place on Saturday if you agree to show up."

John Paul was one of those great cooks who steered clear of the kitchen unless there was an emergency. It had been forever since he had cooked for me alone. We mostly ate at Maddalena's with our friends. Other nights he stayed at my place and we ordered food in. But I wanted him to cook for me all of a sudden. More than I ever had before, I wanted him to myself.

"Just you and me?" I asked.

"I'll make sure we have the entire place to ourselves."

"It's a deal," I said.

When we fell asleep, his arm was wrapped securely around me.

• • •

I was caught completely off guard by Gabriella's invitation. She was having a "small get-together" at her apartment on Friday evening. Mali was going to be there, of course. So were all of our friends. It had been months since I had attended one of our get-togethers with both Mali and John Paul. I knew I couldn't say no, but I decided I wasn't going alone. I called Ariadne.

When Ariadne and I stepped off the train on Ninth Avenue, I felt weak. I was stricken with fear of the unknown. The closer we got to Gabriella's apartment, the slower I walked. When Ariadne stopped to light a cigarillo I thought about going back home.

John Paul was standing outside of Gabriella's building, smoking a cigarette. The cigarette almost fell out of his mouth when he saw Ariadne. He waved, his eyes stuck on her.

"Hello, John Paul," Ariadne said, walking through the door he held open for us.

Gabriella's door was open. When we walked into the apartment I felt a strange, nauseous feeling seize my stomach. I shouldn't have come, I thought. I could feel Mali's presence there.

John Paul made a beeline for the kitchen the minute we entered the apartment. Ariadne rolled her eyes and said she was going to find someplace to dump her coat. I stood alone. A second later John Paul was handing me a tall glass of something bright green. He said it was supposed to be a margarita, but he thought something had gone wrong in the blender. He tried it, pretended to spit it up. I laughed.

Peter called him over to the other side of the room, where he was standing with Mali, looking cornered and bored. John Paul said he'd be right back.

Mali pretended she didn't see me and put her hand on John

Paul's back. He stepped away from her. Her hand dropped. She looked in my direction just as Ariadne came over and squeezed my arm.

"What is this? A margarita?" She took the bright green drink out of my hand. "I'll get you a glass of wine."

"I want a *real* margarita," I said.

"Okay. But first, I'd like you to meet a *real* man."

"I don't want to meet a real man," I protested as she pulled me away. "I'm not single."

"You should be."

I stopped.

She tilted her head and raised her eyebrows. "Follow me. I just met the most interesting person."

I followed her to Gabriella's bedroom. Josh was standing by the window, drinking Budweiser.

"Casey," he said.

"What are you doing here?" I asked.

His face went red. "I was invited."

"How? By who?"

"Hey." He put his beer on the windowsill and started to move past me. "You want me to go?"

Ariadne caught his arm. "Hang on, cowboy. Don't go any-where."

I flashed Ariadne a look. How would she like it if someone tried to set her boyfriend up with another woman? She excused herself with "I owe someone a margarita."

We watched her leave, and then we looked at each other. "I'm sorry. I'm a little overwhelmed right now," I said.

He nodded, picked up his beer again.

"I didn't see a bike—"

"Didn't bring it," he cut me off. "Didn't want to disturb the neighbors."

He was wearing tight jeans and a leather jacket. He leaned against the wall, his free hand jammed deep in his pocket. I was taken back to high school for a minute, when a guy had done something like that and his eyes had been full of me, like no one else in the room existed.

"I should tell you why I'm really here," he said, looking down, then back up at me. "Mali called me."

"She did?"

"I wanted to be able to see you again. It's the only reason why I gave her my number."

"You see me in school."

"I wanted to see you outside of school. Again. And she told me it's hard to know what's happening with you . . . John Paul and you. So I came."

"She didn't say that."

"What's happening with you?" he asked.

"Why do you care what's happening with me?"

"Because it's how I feel."

I didn't know what to say.

"Casey?" he said quietly.

"I don't know what to say."

He nodded. "That's fair. Neither do I."

We stood uncomfortably for a while and it was obvious we wanted to escape each other.

I couldn't involve myself with a student. He seemed genuine, like the real thing, but I didn't trust it.

"Do you want another beer?" I asked.

"Sure. I'll get it," he said.

We walked into the living room, where Peter and John Paul were talking to Dock, who had finally arrived. Dock called out to me, came over, and gave me a hug. He held his hand out to Josh and introduced himself.

Josh smiled. "Josh."

"Did you meet my girlfriend, Polo?"

Josh shook his head and Dock looked around for Polo. "You'll meet her later."

In the kitchen, Mali and Polo were sitting at the table, leaning close and conspiratorially. Polo and Mali had always been friendly. Of everyone in our crew of friends, Polo seemed to like Mali the most.

The conversation stopped when they saw me. I introduced Josh to Polo and hated the way she looked him over like he was for sale or something. Mali grinned at him.

Josh grabbed another beer from the refrigerator. On his way out he almost collided with Gabriella. She watched him walk away.

"I can think of a hundred and one ways to keep that boy happy," Mali said when Josh left the kitchen. "But he didn't even look in my direction. Looks like John Paul may have some competition."

"There's nothing going on there," Gabriella said.

"I know." Mali rolled her eyes. "Casey's too perfect."

"Nobody's perfect," I said.

"You're not perfect?" Polo asked, a little mockery in her voice.

"No," I answered. Polo never needed a reason to mock me. "You just think I am."

Polo lost her smile. "You keep thinking that and have fun with it," she said, standing up. Mali stood up as well and they left the kitchen.

"Ignore them," Gabriella told me as she piled her plate high with potato salad, ham, coleslaw and pickles. Then she smiled sheepishly because she knew she could do no such thing. "Mali doesn't shut up. She thinks she knows everything. Was she always like this?"

"Yes."

"I used to admire her."

I remembered Gabriella wishing she had Mali's legs. "What was that . . . tête-à-tête they were having?"

Gabriella stuffed her mouth with coleslaw and shrugged. "Maybe she was telling Polo about her mother."

"Yeah," I said. "Lobbying for another sympathy vote."

"Well," Gabriella said, casually changing the subject. "Peter and I broke up last night."

"What?"

"We're having problems," she explained, lowering her voice. "With sex. He's not . . . we're not doing it."

"You broke up because you're not having sex?" I asked, incredulous.

"It's not like the punishment-celibacy thing. . . ."

"Punishment celibacy? Is that what you call it?"

"I'm talking about a guy who is great in bed," she said. "Like no other guy I've ever been with. We used to do it twice a day."

"Twice a day?"

"Twice. And now we're hardly doing it at all. Once a week, if I'm lucky. I've tried everything. I even wore heels."

"You're kidding."

"And I started thinking . . . " She stood up and looked into the living room, where Peter was standing by the window. "This is crazy, really, but what if Peter's gay? I keep thinking he might be gay. And you know how I feel about instinct, right? Would that be crazy?"

"I think so."

"You think you know Peter, but you really don't," she said.

"I know he isn't gay."

"Think about it. The guys have been living together for years. They don't lead separate lives. They share everything. And neither one of them wants to get their own place. And now John Paul is infatuated with Mali again, and she probably still dabbles in the gay world. You know, once a thief, always a thief."

Mali had one experience with a woman a couple of months after John Paul and I started dating. I wasn't even sure if I believed her. She would say anything to get his attention. I walked away from Gabriella, disturbed by the idea that she thought John Paul was still "infatuated" with Mali. Gabriella followed me.

"It's funny you should say that," I said, spotting Mali taking a sip from John Paul's drink. "The thing about Mali being a thief."

We stared at Mali for a minute. Gabriella sighed.

"I guess the gay theory is a little extreme," Gabriella said.

"Yeah, well."

"Peter likes women," she continued. "He thinks you're sexy."

I looked at Peter. He was watching us. When he saw me looking at him, he winked. He thought I was sexy?

"I went through this with John Paul," I said, trying to shake the idea of Peter finding me sexy out of my head. "I'm still going through it. The sex issue is—"

"It's different." Gabriella cut me off.

"It's not that different."

"It is," she said abruptly. "I don't want your advice, Casey."

"Sorry." I was surprised by her tone.

She took a deep breath and shook her head. "No. I'm sorry."

We didn't say anything for a long time.

Then Mali laughed at something John Paul said and I

cringed. I felt like it should have been me laughing. It used to be me. John Paul and I used to talk. We used to know each other. Suddenly, we were like an old married couple. We didn't talk and we didn't have sex. The prettiest girl at the party was usurping his attention.

"Aren't you surprised Josh showed up?" Gabriella asked.

"Yes." Josh was talking to Ariadne, Peter and Dock in a corner of the room.

"He's just got it," Gabriella said. "You know what *it* I'm talking about, right?"

Of course I did. Standing there next to Peter and Dock, and among my friends, Josh looked like a fish out of water. Wrong clothes, wrong hair, wrong beer. But no one could take their eyes off him, including John Paul. Josh stood sexy, drank Bud sexy, laughed at corny jokes sexy, wore his leather jacket sexy and looked at me from the corner of his eye sexy.

Yes. He was watching me. Every few minutes he would look around for me and find me and smile.

There's a history of women who made bad choices about men. I was one of them. The only man on my mind at that moment was John Paul, and how close Mali was standing next to him.

"Excuse me for a second," I said to Gabriella.

I went into the kitchen and leaned against the sink. I closed my eyes.

"How's it going?" Peter asked. He was standing in front of me. He smiled, showing off a mouth of perfectly straight white teeth. He didn't look like a man who'd just been dumped by his girlfriend, but then again, he didn't have the kind of face that I'd call an open book either.

"Whatever you're thinking is probably accurate," I said.

"I'm not thinking anything very good."

"Well ..."

"*You* could have stayed with us if she refused to leave."

"Right," I said. "I could have handed her my parents' lease as well. Just give her everything."

He laughed. Then he said, "Gabriella say anything to you?"

"We spoke briefly," I replied uncomfortably. Peter and I were friends. I liked him. Despite his tendency toward machismo, he was basically an okay guy. But I didn't want to talk about the breakup with him. It didn't seem right to talk about it with both of them.

"Did she tell you that we're ... we decided to take a break for a minute?" All of the sadness he'd been hiding showed up on his face.

"I'm sure it'll work out," I said sympathetically. "In a couple of seconds."

He grimaced. Bad humor is not the answer to a broken heart.

A confession: part of me found solace in knowing someone was feeling crappier about their love life than I was.

"I'm tired," he admitted.

In all of the years I'd known him, I never heard Peter say anything like that.

"You can't let this get to you," I said. "Seven years."

"Yeah." He looked at me like I said something profound. "Doesn't that seem really long to you?"

I opened my mouth but thought better of continuing. I was afraid I'd say the wrong thing again. With men, you may think you're saying the absolute right thing, but they hear it differently. Seven years to me meant hold on. Seven years to him meant he'd wasted a lot of time.

He said, "I always thought she'd be around. I thought our love was unconditional. Nothing would break us up."

"Peter ..."

"You look good," he said. His eyes canvassed my body, making me feel awkward.

"Thanks." I inched away from him.

"I really admire you for sticking it out with John Paul." He inched away with me.

"Am I interrupting?" Mali asked, eyebrows raised like she'd walked in on something newsworthy.

"No," we said in unison, alerting her that she had. Peter picked up a glass from the table and poured himself a drink.

Mali patted him on the shoulder. "Glad you came."

He smiled and nodded, but didn't look at her.

"Hope you're having a nice time." She smiled at me.

I knew that trick. The one where she pretended to be concerned about my well-being in front of my friends.

"I am." I was cold, curt.

"Good." She leaned against the counter next to me.

I told Peter I'd talk to him later, and then I left the kitchen.

John Paul and I were standing in the living room talking to Dock when Mali came out of the kitchen. She rubbed Dock's arm and asked how he was doing. Dock moved away from her, said he was doing fine.

"You liked London?" he asked.

"Loved it," she said.

"You were there for a long time," he pointed out

"About three months."

Dock nodded. "Long time."

"I needed to find myself." She laughed. "Going to another country is the best way to do that. You can be whoever you want to be in another country. And England is perfect. You don't have to learn a new language."

"I hope you found whoever you were looking for," John Paul said. I detected the bitterness in his voice right away. We all did. Dock took a deep breath and looked away as though he was fed up. I thought he was going to walk away from the conversation.

"Are you still angry with me for leaving?" Mali asked evenly.

"Still?" I said, cheeks flaring.

John Paul shifted his weight from one foot to the other and looked at me like I should know better. "I was never angry."

Mali nodded, eyes narrowed, a slight smile playing on her lips. We all knew he was lying. We heard the anger. Very subtly, Dock touched my elbow. It was a signal. He wanted me to walk away with him, to leave them to their drama. I couldn't.

"You're just jealous," Mali told John Paul. "Because while I was in London exploring new and exciting things, you all were here. Stuck here with the same parties, same drinks and same people. Standing around, listening to everyone else's stories, wishing you were somewhere else."

He loved this? I wondered. And Dock said, "Like now, listening to you. You're right. I'd rather be in London."

Mali didn't look at Dock.

Polo came over, kissed him on the cheek, said she wanted another drink. Mali smiled at him then, for Polo's benefit. Dock excused himself, and Mali followed behind them.

I was aware of the way John Paul and I had spent our time while Mali was away: standing around, drinking, listening to other people's conversations. Everything had become habit for us. Meeting at Maddalena's. Brunch on Saturdays. My celibacy.

And there was Mali. Returned. Coming out of the kitchen with Polo, pretending to listen to her, stopping, staring at him. The look in her eyes scared me. So intense, screaming: *You have to love me!* I looked at him, too, feeling the same way, screaming: *No, you have to love me!*

But I started to wonder how he could love a woman who wouldn't let him touch her for over three months. I wondered how I could love a man who hadn't bothered to try to change my mind.

"You want something from the kitchen?" he asked and I shook my head.

He disappeared from my side and Dock came over with a plate of nachos and salsa.

"She doesn't have to be here," he said.

"She could be *there*. At Peter and John Paul's."

"True." He nodded. "And then what?"

We both looked at Josh without meaning to. Josh was keeping an eye on me. Dock turned away, chuckled.

"Look at that," Dock said softly. And then he walked away.

I looked at Josh again. He had been quiet most of the evening, listening patiently to my friends babble. He nodded politely, swallowed his beer, and searched the room until he found me again.

As the night wore on, the only people who seemed to notice that Josh was constantly looking for me were Ariadne and Dock. Every time Josh and I had a fleeting eye connection, Ariadne and Dock turned up somewhere in my line of vision, eyebrows raised in interest. I swear they would make good parents. Their kids would never get away with anything.

"Cute sweater," I said when I caught up with Ariadne outside of the bathroom.

"Ninety-nine cents." She twirled around in circles so I'd get a better look at her lime-green sweater. Then she looked at me again and smiled. "There's something I want to show you. Come with me to the bedroom."

"Why can't you show me right here?"

"Because it's in the bedroom."

I followed her into Gabriella's bedroom. Josh was staring out the window again. Ariadne introduced us to each other as though we'd never met. Josh grinned at her, really enjoying her for a second. Ariadne winked at him before she left.

"You remind me of my dad," I said. "He always manages to find the one interesting window at a party."

"Where is he?"

"Los Angeles with my mom."

"Film business?"

"Sort of."

He nodded.

"I'm sorry," I said.

He stuffed his hands in his pockets. "Sorry I came?"

"No." I meant it. "I'm sorry you aren't enjoying yourself."

"I like Ariadne," he said.

"So do I."

"I like Dock and Polo."

"Polo?"

He nodded. "They're together, but they're different."

They were together, and they were different. Dock was a better person.

Josh said, "Ariadne told me Mali's his ex."

I nodded.

"That's why she called me. To try to stir things up."

I shrugged. "I guess."

"He tried to set me up with her."

"You're kidding."

"I think it was his way of trying to piss her off . . . " He stopped and stared at the door behind me.

"Can I talk to you?" John Paul asked.

I didn't turn around to look at him. My eyes settled on Josh apologetically. Josh smiled just enough for me to know it was a smile.

"Talk to you later," he said and left the room.

I leaned against the window and stared out at the sidewalk. John Paul put his hand on my shoulder, kissed my neck.

"Why are you setting my friends up on dates?" I asked.

John Paul raised his eyebrows. "Mali's your friend now?"

"I meant Josh."

"Josh told you?" He frowned. "Why would he tell you that?"

"He told me."

"I didn't know you had that kind of relationship. I thought he was just a student."

"He's a friend," I said.

"Oh?"

"Why did you try to set them up?" I asked. "Are you trying to call her bluff?"

"No." He shook his head. "It's not a big deal."

"Why are you so angry if it's not a big deal?"

"I'm not angry," he said. "Who's feeding you this crap? Ariadne? That kid?"

"Mali pointed out the anger," I told him. "And I see it."

"What's going on? You won't look at me, you won't talk to me . . . " He closed his eyes for a second and shook his head. "I've barely said three words to her because I'm afraid you'll get mad. I'm trying my damnedest not to be alone with her. Not to look at her, not to touch her by accident. And every time I turn around, this guy is there. What's that about? Is there something I should know?"

"Don't turn this around and try to implicate me in something," I warned.

"I'm not. I just want to know if you're attracted to him."

"He's my student."

"And your friend."

"Our friend," I corrected.

"You still haven't answered the question," he said.

"I'm not going to answer it, okay? It's a stupid question."

He stared at me for a long time. "Fine."

"Fine."

"There's nothing going on here," he said.

There was a lot going on, as far as I was concerned. He just didn't see it. That's the thing about men. Attention directed at *them* is perfectly okay. No matter where it's coming from.

"What are you so uncomfortable about?" he wanted to know. "You think we're going to get undressed in the middle of the room, in front of all of our friends, and—"

"Fuck?" I asked.

He flushed. After a minute he asked, "Are we still on for tomorrow?"

"A romantic dinner to celebrate our anniversary?" I mocked excitement. "Sure. Why wouldn't we be?"

His jaw clenched. "Peter has his dad's car this week. He'll give us a ride to Brooklyn."

"No," I said. "Josh and I are going in the same direction."

John Paul managed to look like I had insulted him and he was going to be a good sport about it. But twenty minutes later, when Ariadne said she had "places to go and people to see," John Paul grabbed his coat and left behind her. Without a word to anyone. He never liked to be the first to arrive or leave a party.

Peter tried to hang around, tried to be the last to go, but Gabriella asked Josh and I to stick around until he got the picture. Eventually he did get the picture. About ten minutes

later. He left when he realized Josh and I weren't going anywhere.

I suggested we start to clean up. Suddenly, Mali decided she
needed to go out "for a minute." She disappeared.

Gabriella was relieved everyone was gone. She said she was
tired and she'd clean up in the morning. Josh told her he
would take care of it. She hesitated, and then she smiled mis-
chievously at me, as though there were a plan we hadn't let her
in on. She asked if we'd turn out the lights when we left.

Josh helped me wash the dishes and put the leftover food
away. I felt there was something he wanted to say to me, but I
didn't encourage it. When I came out of the bathroom, ready
to leave, he was sitting in the living room, drinking a beer. He
set the beer on a napkin and stood up.

"About me and her . . . "

"It doesn't matter," I said.

"I told you why I gave her my number," he continued.

I nodded.

"She has her sights set on someone else anyway." He smiled.
I didn't. "And I'd rather go out with you."

"I have a boyfriend," I reminded him.

"But are you happy?" he asked.

I didn't answer.

He sat down again, picked up his beer and offered it to me. I
sat next to him, took the beer, tasted it. He leaned toward me. I
stood up and paced the room with his Bud.

"What is it?" he asked impatiently. "Are you not interested
because I'm young, white, or working-class? Because the thing
is, I'm twenty-three. There's not a huge age difference. I can't
change that I'm white, and my mom brought me up to believe
there's no shame in being working-class."

I stopped pacing. "Have you considered that it might be because I'm your professor and I can lose my job?"

"Is that what's stopping you? I'll drop the class."

"Josh." I sat next to him again, trying to remember the speech I had prepared after I started my job and Zabrowski went over the rules for professor-student etiquette. I never used it, so it was pretty rusty. "You have a crush on me because I teach you something you're really interested in. And you can't drop a class you need to graduate because you have a crush. You see one side of me twice a week, and I have my guard up. You're seeing a side of me that isn't real. It's a facade. You could get to know me and not like me at all."

He stared at me for a long time, and then he smiled. "You're just making this more challenging."

I handed him the beer. "I'm not trying to."

"Well, the part of you I saw tonight was real," he said. "The part I saw in the Polka Dot was real. I like that part. You don't have to make stuff up to let me down easy. I know you got your degree from Columbia, and here I am taking a couple of classes at this shitty school—"

"I don't think I'm better than you."

"I applied twice to Columbia's film program," he said. "And I was rejected."

"That has nothing to do with this. I'm just a film teacher. An adjunct."

"You have the degree. You have a future if you want it. I bet you have a brilliant script in your apartment somewhere."

"I have several brilliant scripts in my apartment somewhere, but they aren't mine. My scripts suck. My ideas suck."

"I don't believe that."

"I wrote a script for my thesis," I admitted. "I didn't finish it. My advisor told me I didn't have a knack for it. He said I wasn't original. He said everyone loves movies, but only a select few can make them."

"He was a jerk," Josh said quietly.

"I've never told that to anyone." I slouched back into the sofa, amazed that I'd told him. "He called me scattered and distant, and he said I should consider a career in teaching because I'd never make it in film. He accepted my script because he liked me. I never contradicted him the way other students did. So I got the degree and he called Zabrowski and got me a job."

Why am I telling him all of this? I asked myself. Why am I coming clean with a twenty-three-year-old student?

"I used to watch you and Ariadne," he said. "When I found out you were a teacher in the film department it blew me away. I went to all of the department meetings because I wanted to see you. I loved the way you walked into meetings late, leaned over and asked someone what you missed, then walked out again. You were funny and cute."

Funny and cute. Is that a good thing?

I felt him leaning closer to me. He hesitated when I didn't respond. I stood up. "Somehow, at twenty-nine I didn't expect to be funny and cute," I said.

He stood up as well. "It was a compliment."

"I have to go," I told him.

"I'll walk you to the train."

"No. That's okay."

"I won't take no for an answer," he said.

I watched him carry his beer bottle to the kitchen. He waited for me by the door as I turned out the lights for Gabriella.

On our way to the elevator he turned back slightly.

I moved forward.

Our kiss was so brief it barely happened.

• • •

John Paul was standing in the lobby, waiting for me. He held
an unlit cigarette in his hand, rolling it over his fingers as he
watched us with an expression of impatient boredom. Josh
and I stopped and stared back at him.

John Paul said, "I'm going to take Casey home. You want to
share a cab with us?"

Josh declined, sensing the offer wasn't sincere. He waved at
me, glancing at John Paul self-consciously. I watched him disappear through the lobby doors.

"You did a good job of making me feel like shit up there,"
John Paul said.

"Now you know how I feel most of the time."

"C'mon," he groaned. "What am I supposed to do, ignore
her?"

"*Yes* comes to mind."

"Well, I can't."

"Why not?"

"Why can't we just be us?" he asked. "Mali is a part of our
crew. She always has been. Why can't we just leave it at that?"

"There are so many reasons, I don't even know where to begin."

"This is you," he said. "You're the one letting her come between us."

"Yes. And it was once and it was a long time ago," I snapped.
"It was a mistake and you were stupid."

"Jesus, Casey." He looked pained. "I'm not with her, am I?
You don't . . . She doesn't have to exist for you."

"But she does," I told him. "She very much does."

He sighed, covered his mouth with his hand. "Do you want
this to work?" he asked. And then he shook his head and said,

"I'm not here to argue with you. I just wanted to be here when you came down. I just want . . . I want us to be what we are."

I said, "I won't share you with her."

"Let me take you home." He reached for me. I pulled away.

"I want to go home alone."

"I thought we were good."

He couldn't know that every time they were in the same room together I thought the same thing: *I thought we were good.*

"We were working it out," he said. "It was better."

"And then she came back."

He swallowed hard. He nodded. "Give me tomorrow," he said. "She won't be at my place tomorrow."

Ten

It had been a while since John Paul and I had dinner at his apartment. Peter and Gabriella were usually there, or we had some previous engagement with the gang. As I packed an overnight bag I felt sanguine. We were sacrificing the gang, Mali, and our Saturday night at Maddalena's for each other.

John Paul greeted me at the door with a tall glass of champagne. He kissed me gently as we stepped into the apartment, which he had succeeded in transforming into a romantic refuge equipped with candles, incense and Miles Davis's *Kind of Blue* playing softly in the background.

"What do you smell?" he asked, heading for the kitchen to check on something.

"Garlic," I called out. "Butter."

"The better to eat lobster with, my dear."

"I love lobster."

"I know."

I put my bag on the floor as he carried a bucket of ice and the rest of the champagne into the room. He smiled when he saw the bag.

We drank champagne and ate a Caesar salad that John Paul prepared at the table. The CD changed from Miles Davis to Marvin Gaye to Roberta Flack, and we talked about what made a great love song great, and we argued whether lobster could be considered an aphrodisiac.

When Roberta came on singing "Let It Be Me," John Paul stood up and asked me to dance with him. We danced slowly, tentatively. When the song finished he kissed me.

And then the buzzer rang.

Our eyes met. John Paul sighed. I'm sure we were thinking the same thing: Mali had gone too far.

"Don't," I said.

He stared at me, and then he looked at the white candles burning around us. White candles are supposed to ward off evil, I thought.

"Two lobsters gave up their lives so we can be together tonight," I told him, appealing to his compassionate side. One of the most touching things about that evening was that John Paul had a fear of boiling lobsters and hearing their screams.

"Four," he corrected, looking at me again.

"There you go," I said.

He pulled me closer to him and buried his face in my hair. He probably would have let her buzz all night if the doorbell hadn't rung. Damn buildings without doormen. We pulled apart.

"You had no idea?" I asked.

"Not a clue."

We were surprised to see Peter and Gabriella standing in the doorway. Especially since Peter lived there and had a key.

"Hope we aren't interrupting," Peter slurred as he walked past us and entered the apartment.

"I'm sorry," Gabriella said. "He's drunk. I told him I'm going to visit my grandmother in Boston and he doesn't believe me. He thinks I have a new boyfriend or something." She looked around. "Everything's so romantic."

"Yes, well. It's supposed to be a romantic evening."

"I really didn't know."

I shrugged, watched Peter lead John Paul away while he babbled in his ear.

"I'm sorry about this," Gabriella whispered. "It's so stupid."

"It's not your fault." Deep down I was blaming Gabriella. I couldn't help it.

"When he stopped by my apartment he was already toasted," she explained. "He started crying and begging me not to go away. He thinks I'm going to see some guy in Boston. *I wish.* He said he left the house without cash and someone tried to mug him. It was a mess. I couldn't say no when he asked me to listen. I guess he wants to plead his case, try to work things out. I don't know. Since Mali's at my place . . . I had no idea you were here. He didn't explain that part until he buzzed, and then it was too late. I've never seen him like this before. I thought if I could at least get him home, into a shower . . . Oh, the candles are so pretty."

I didn't want to be a bitch about the whole thing and ask her to take him back to her place. You know how that is. I couldn't expect her to spend the night with her ex-boyfriend, and I imagined Peter waking up in a gutter somewhere with a tragic hangover and the memory of me pitching a fit and kicking him out of his own apartment. It wasn't fair, but there was hardly any choice in the matter. And John Paul didn't seem like he cared so much that they were there. He certainly didn't ask them to leave.

"I'll keep him in his room," Gabriella promised as we watched Peter pour himself a glass of champagne. He spilled some of the champagne and John Paul laughed at whatever stupid thing he said. "I swear, I'll keep him in his room," Gabriella repeated. "Peter!"

Peter and John Paul stopped laughing and looked at us. Gabriella motioned for Peter to follow her upstairs.

John Paul waited for the bedroom door to close. He shook his head and picked up his glass. "Hungry?" he asked me.

Just as we sat down to resume our romantic dinner, the doorbell rang again. We stared at the door. I knew who it was. I wondered what had taken her so long.

John Paul sighed deeply and answered the door.

"Is Peter okay?" Mali walked into the apartment without an invitation.

"Don't you have a job?" I asked.

She looked at me, slightly amused. "I work days," she answered. She walked around the room, checking out the champagne, the table, the candles. She glimpsed my bag on the floor and hesitated by it. Then she said, "What are you trying to do, Paulie boy, burn the house down?"

"Mali." John Paul sounded exhausted, like he'd been chasing a two-year-old around the living room all day. "You have to leave."

Mali wasn't sure she heard him correctly. She looked at him, stared. She pointed upstairs. "Let me see if Gabriella wants to come with me."

"Really." He blocked her way up the stairs. "You have to go."

She didn't budge for a minute, and then she moved away and looked at my bag again.

"Okay," she conceded. "Tell Gabriella I stopped by."

When she left, he locked the door and leaned against it. "I'm sorry," he said.

I stared at the floor, happy he'd thrown her out. He walked over to me and started to rub the back of my neck.

"Where were we?" he asked.

He kissed me again, roughly. He was trying too hard and I sensed he was preoccupied. I pulled back a little, to lighten it up, but he grabbed the back of my head, mashing our lips together.

"Stop," I said, wrenching away from him.

He stopped, but he wouldn't look me in the eye. He went into the kitchen, opened the refrigerator door and stared inside.

"You want to go home?" he asked.

"I want to finish the evening."

He took a bottle of water out of the refrigerator and drank from it.

I went into the kitchen and put my hand on his chest and moved closer to him. He watched me. He didn't respond. I stood on my toes to kiss him. He pulled his head back slightly and lowered his eyes.

"Let's save this," he said.

"Why?"

Just then Peter's bedroom door opened and Gabriella came out. Peter rushed out after her. "I love you, Gabriella!" he cried.

Gabriella ran down the stairs and came into the kitchen. "I'm sorry," she said. "Really sorry. He's being a jerk."

"But I love you!" Peter screamed, dropping to his knees. I

was embarrassed for him until John Paul started to laugh and I
realized he was acting. Peter also started to laugh and Gabriella
rolled her eyes and gave him the finger.

"Jerks," she mumbled.

John Paul went upstairs and helped Peter to his feet. They
said something, looked down at us, laughed some more.

"Hey, girls," Peter called out. "Wanna go for a drive? You up
for that?"

"Who would get in a car with you?" Gabriella shouted back.

John Paul was rubbing the rim of his glass with a finger, listening to Peter babble nonsensically, laughing.

The thing about boys is they're pretty much convinced it's
the thought that counts more than the actual outcome. Just
because the dinner was prepared and the candles were lit
didn't mean he'd made it up to me. He thought he had.

The other thing about boys is they're usually more loyal to
their friends.

"I don't mind going for a drive," I told Gabriella. "Maybe if
they get some air ... "

Gabriella shrugged.

I said, "Mali came by looking for you."

"She did?"

I nodded. "So the evening's ruined already. Maybe if we go
out ... "

"Okay," she agreed reluctantly.

The car, a black Lexus, belonged to Peter's father. He was car-
sitting while his parents were on vacation. I sat in the backseat
with Gabriella because she didn't want to sit in back with Peter. When John Paul pulled away from the building, Peter
pulled out a pipe and began packing the bowl with marijuana.

He lit it and started to smoke, then passed it to John Paul, who declined.

Pot made John Paul worry about laundry and washing dishes. He would take long showers and fix things that had been broken for months. He would take out garbage and start to exercise, and then he would eat too much.

Pot helped me forget I was feeling lousy.

I took the pipe from Peter and smoked. I held the smoke in my chest for as long as I could stand it, and then I coughed so hard I thought I would lose a lung. Gabriella patted my back and asked if I was okay. I nodded as a spasm of coughs hit me again. She started to laugh at me, and then she took the pipe and smoked. She started to choke as well.

Peter hollered with laughter.

"It's been a while," I told him between chokes.

We continued to take turns until a police car whizzed by. I straightened in my seat and watched it disappear ahead of us.

"Police," I said.

"Shit," John Paul said softly. "Maybe we should stop for a while."

John Paul parked the car on a side street in Lower Manhattan and we went to a Greek diner a block away. We sat in a booth near a window. Gabriella sat next to John Paul; they shared a menu. Peter and I sat across from them, sharing a menu as well.

I realized the pot was affecting me strangely and I started to wonder if Peter had mixed something else with it. I felt horny. Peter was starting to look good to me. I was noticing his long, muscular neck, broad chest and chiseled jawbone. He was sitting close to me, looking at the menu. I could feel his breath on my cheek and his leg touching my leg. A couple of times he looked at me and we made eye contact and I felt a dull pain in my chest.

"What the hell is happening to me?" I kept asking myself. And John Paul kept leaning toward me, saying, "What?"

Peter and Gabriella ordered gyro platters. John Paul and I agreed to share a salad. We ate quickly when our food arrived. Peter and Gabriella finished eating first. The waitress came by to pick up their empty plates. Gabriella grabbed her plate out of the waitress's hands and set it back on the table with a loud thud, declaring she wasn't finished. The stunned look on the waitress's face was priceless. John Paul and Peter started to laugh hysterically.

"I'm so high," Gabriella murmured as she ripped off a piece of Peter's pita bread and mopped up the last bits of yogurt and lettuce on her plate.

John Paul paid for the meal when we were ready to leave, anxious to avoid a splitting-the-bill scenario with Peter and Gabriella. He held the door open and ushered us out.

When we reached the car, Peter and I grabbed the back-door handle at the same time. His hand covered mine and I jerked away from him involuntarily. For a brief moment, there was a heavy silence and we all stared at one another.

"What's wrong?" Gabriella stared at me over the roof of the car.

"Nothing," I said. My voice was thick.

Peter's hand was warm and soft. The feel of it sent a chill through me. I glanced at him. Our eyes met briefly, and then he opened the back door.

"You want to sit up front with me?" John Paul asked.

I shook my head.

Peter slid into the passenger seat next to John Paul.

Before he started the car again, John Paul looked at Gabriella in the rearview mirror. "What next?"

"Would you take me home?" Gabriella said.

Peter crashed on the sofa the minute we walked into the apartment. John Paul checked their messages. I brought my bag upstairs.

John Paul's room wasn't much bigger than a walk-in closet. It was such a New York City bedroom. Three thousand dollars a month for a spacious, rent-controlled duplex, yet the actual size of the bedroom was no bigger than a fitting room at Saks Fifth Avenue.

There was a bed, a dresser and an ironing board, which was set up in the middle of the room, partially blocking the doorway. All of the dresser drawers were open, clothes falling out of them. His room was a complete disaster and his closet was a complete contradiction to that disaster. All of his suits hung neatly in clothes bags, several inches apart.

I changed into my pajamas and waited for him. When he came up, he smiled and lay on the bed next to me. He flung an arm over my lap and buried his face in a pillow. He mumbled something like "I hope you had a nice time," and then he was fast asleep.

Eleven

The next time we saw Mali, we were at Maddalena's. We were standing at the bar with Peter, Gabriella, Dock and Polo.

She said, "Casey, I'm sorry I interrupted whatever was going on Saturday. I was just checking up on Peter. He was distraught and I wanted to lend Gabriella a hand. I didn't know you were going to be there."

"You don't ever have to check up on me," Peter told her.

Still, John Paul put his hand on my back and thanked her for apologizing. That was another trick I knew: the apology-in-front-of-my-boyfriend-and-his-friends trick. Now he thought she was a saint.

Days passed and Mali's friend in Brooklyn didn't materialize. I was surprised Gabriella didn't talk about kicking her out of the apartment.

"She's so plastic I could take her shopping and never pull out a credit card," Gabriella told me. "But she's a good person. She just has a few issues."

As a group, we didn't stop meeting at Maddalena's, which meant I saw more of Mali than I cared to and Gabriella saw Peter. It became painfully clear to both Peter and me that we had something in common. We wanted things to be the way they used to be.

And every time Gabriella, Polo or John Paul laughed at something Mali said, enjoyed another story about London or remembered some great memory they shared, I started to regret that so much of my time was spent hating her and fearing her and wishing she were dead. I regretted that everything was so complicated, regretted that she was my enemy, not my friend. I did want things to be the way John Paul thought they could be. But I knew they couldn't. Because Mali didn't want it. She hadn't come back for that.

Part of me wished I hadn't let her leave my apartment. I was sorry I let her loose on the streets of Manhattan, because Gabriella couldn't keep the kind of tabs on her I could have kept. And it wasn't that I feared they would deliberately keep their nights out together from me. It wasn't that I was worried about being left out.

Mali had an edge on me by being in Manhattan.

There was always the threat of quick stops at the diner on Ninth Avenue for midnight chats when she and Gabriella couldn't sleep, afterwork snacks at the Thai restaurant on Eighth, and early-morning coffee at the deli before John Paul and Peter went to work. Impromptu meetings I wouldn't be invited to because they weren't planned, and I lived too far away to join them.

All of those possibilities exhausted me. I thought: If I have
to spend one more evening worrying about Mali I am going to
kill someone.

It was Saturday. John Paul was meeting me at my apartment.
We were planning to spend the evening alone. But when I came
home from a brief visit to my office because I left test papers
there that I needed to grade, two pizza boxes on the kitchen
table greeted me. Peter and Mali were rolling joints on the sofa
and John Paul was watching them while he smoked a cigarette.

"I brought dinner," Peter said. "And Mali. Gabriella's at
work."

It's a very bad idea to have the same friends as your
boyfriend. There are no boundaries.

I grabbed a beer from the refrigerator and drank it right
there, with the door open. My heart was pumping savagely and
I needed to calm down. I thought a beer would help. It didn't.
It made me feel worse.

John Paul came into the kitchen to explain. He said, "I
didn't invite her."

I nodded, staring inside the refrigerator.

"He was going to see Gabriella, but Mali was there. I was
just as surprised as you are when she came to the door."

"Okay," I said. "I'm disappointed. Don't ask me not to be."

Peter handed me a joint when I sat next to him. I avoided
looking at John Paul and concentrated on getting high. Mali
started to tell us a story about a woman and her car in London,
and John Paul laughed. After a while, Peter stretched out on
the sofa and drifted off to sleep while I ate a couple of slices of
pizza.

Infidelity has nothing to do with sex and everything to do with determination. Don't get me wrong. There are plenty of one-night stands between spoken-fors at the spur of the moment that are all about a pair of tight jeans, a well-placed hand and a clean bathroom. But destructive infidelity, the infidelity that gets him to look you in the eye and lie, is about a woman who focused every minute of her life on making him feel like he was the only man on earth.

"Mali invited us out for a drink," John Paul told me some time before midnight.

"No. Thanks."

"She wants to talk."

I eyed him carefully. "So."

"I think we should talk to her."

"Do you?"

He proceeded delicately, "I want to talk to her."

John Paul wasn't stupid. Really. He was a good sort of person. Mali used to say he was the type of guy who never suspected anyone of anything, the complete opposite of me. Mali used to say John Paul wouldn't know a girl was trying to get him into bed until she had his pants unzipped and his penis in her mouth. It was a flaw. Like a pull in a new pair of linen pants or a scratch on a vinyl album.

Usually, I'm patient when it comes to flaws.

"Let's end this," I said. "This whole stupid thing. Let's just say we tried and failed."

"What the hell are you talking about?"

"Me. You. Her."

"Why?" he asked. "What are you so bent out of shape about? Something happened with her mother and she wants to talk. To us. Not me alone. Us."

"I don't want to hear about her mother. You go hear about her mother. Don't you see what she's doing? She's looking for sympathy. And she's using this thing with her mother, this pregnancy, to get your attention."

"It's deeper than that," he said.

"Deeper than that? Oh, John Paul."

He shook his head. "I have hardly spent a minute alone with her ... "

"How many minutes alone have you spent with me?" I asked.

"I haven't counted," he said. "But if I could rack up frequent-flyer miles for the amount of time I spend with you alone, I'd be a happy man."

"You aren't funny," I said quietly.

"The point is," he sighed, "I spend a lot of alone-time with you, Casey. I'm not asking a lot here."

I shut my eyes. "Go away," I said. "Be with her."

He mashed his teeth. "You mean that?"

"Of course I mean it," I snapped.

"Casey," he groaned. "I don't want her. She's just my friend."

"Then don't go," I demanded. "Don't ever see her again."

"Don't tell me what to do."

"I'm not telling you what to do."

"Okay." He shook his head, exasperated. Did he have a right to be exasperated? "I won't go. I'll tell her you don't ever want me to see her again."

"You know what?" I sighed heavily. "Go. Just get out. I don't want to see *you* again."

He stood there and waited for me to take it back. I wouldn't.

• • •

The telephone rang in the middle of the night. I was in bed, but I wasn't sleeping.

"I can't sleep," John Paul said quietly. "I can't stop thinking about you."

"It's after two," I said coldly.

"Do you want company?" he asked.

"No."

There was a long silence. I could hear him breathing.

"Did you mean it?" he asked.

"I think . . . " I hesitated. "I don't know."

"Don't hate me," he said.

"I don't hate you." The sad thing was that I didn't.

"I want to be with you. In every way."

"John Paul . . . " I don't know what I was going to say, but it didn't matter. I didn't say it. And all he said was "I'm sorry."

"Hang up," I said and he did.

I had to do something really melodramatic once we hung up, so I got out of bed, drank a bottle of Merlot and listened to Nina Simone. I wanted him to come over and get into bed with me and tell me he loved me. But there was the matter of pride and jealousy, and not letting him off too easy.

When the wine was finished, I took two aspirins and drank three glasses of water to avoid a hangover in the morning. Then I finished the rest of the cold pizza, and played Solitaire on my laptop for an hour.

Eventually, the screen became a blur. I forced myself to get up and go into my bedroom. I fell on the bed and the next thing I knew it was morning and the phone was ringing obnoxiously in my ear. I grabbed it, expecting it to be John Paul.

"Hi." It was Ariadne.

"What time is it?" I asked.

"One."

"I slept until one?"

"Apparently."

"Shit," I groaned.

"What?"

"I didn't want to sleep so late."

"Wanna go to Bobo's tonight?" she asked. "Dock's working and I haven't heard from you in a few days."

"I'm not sure."

"Why aren't you sure?"

"Uh. Can I get back to you?"

"No," she said. "I'll be at Bobo's by nine."

"Can you hold a sec?" It was my call waiting. I thought it was John Paul.

"She didn't come home." It was Gabriella.

"Who didn't come home?"

"Who do you think?"

Don't jump to conclusions, I told myself. Don't think the worst. Because the worst would mean they're dead, or hurt, and not in bed together.

Please, God, I thought, don't let them be in bed together.

I took a couple of deep breaths and stared at the telephone. "Are you sure?"

"I live there. There's only one sofa bed and it wasn't used."

But he just called me. He was home, alone, when he called me. He wanted to come over.

"Listen, I'm not home." She sounded rushed and I realized she was on a pay phone.

"Where are you?"

"I'm on my way to Boston." Her voice cracked. I remembered something about a visit to see her grandmother. "And I am not happy about leaving her my apartment. But I don't have a choice, do I? She has a fucking key and I don't know where she is."

"But—"

"And you can't tell her that I told you about this. I have to work with her when I get back."

"Wait a minute . . . " I was annoyed all of a sudden.

"I really have to go, sweetie. I just wanted to give you a heads-up."

I sat stunned for a while. He had called me. I was sure I hadn't made that up. He wanted to come over. He wanted to see me. Why didn't I have caller ID?

When I hung up, the phone rang. I heard Ariadne humming on the other line.

"Oh. Sorry," I said. I forgot she'd been holding.

"Did I tell you what happened to Shakespeare last week?" Ariadne asked. "We canceled *one* of the *nine* Shakespeare courses we offer and the department was in an uproar on Thursday. I don't know why. No one ever wanted to teach it, and it always ended up being canceled because there weren't enough students—"

"That was Gabriella," I interrupted.

"So?"

I blurted, "Mali didn't come home. She took John Paul out for a drink last night and she didn't make it home."

There was a long silence. Then, "Why did she take him out?"

"She wanted to talk to him."

"Why didn't you go with them?"

"I'll kill them," I said fiercely. "I swear to God I'll kill them."

"Don't overreact," she warned.

"I let her back in."

"Calm down," she soothed. "This is what she wants you to do. Don't give her this power. Don't be a victim."

"*Please,* don't give me that Larry crap right now," I said. "I can't deal with that shit right now."

She was silent for a long time.

"I'm sorry," I said and sat on my bed.

"Do you want to tell me what happened?"

"No." My voice cracked.

"Don't cry," she said.

I nodded but couldn't promise anything.

"I knew this—" she started.

"Don't say it," I pleaded.

"Okay, I won't say it."

We didn't say anything.

"You have to let him go." Silence wasn't Ariadne's forte.

"How can I let him go? I've loved him ever since I met him."

"Larry tells me this wonderful thing," she said slowly. "You can always start again tomorrow."

"Larry's a dick," I snapped. "Can he tell me how I get five years back?"

"You don't. Just don't waste five more."

"He's fucking her, isn't he?" I said. "I let her win."

"Win what? What are you talking about?"

"Shit, that's my call waiting again."

"It's probably him. Call me if it isn't—"

I clicked off with Ariadne before she could finish. It wasn't John Paul. It was a wrong number. I sounded so distraught, the person on the other end asked if I was okay. I was struck by her kindness and wondered what she would do if I asked her to stop by and comfort me.

"I'm okay, thank you," I said and hung up before she did.

I dialed John Paul's number and let it ring and ring until his answering machine picked up. I hung up and dialed again. Eventually he will pick up, I told myself. Whether he's home or not.

I kept calling and hanging up just like it was the most logical thing in the world to do. I paced my bedroom, then sat down on the bed again and took a deep breath. The thing I feared most was happening. And I wasn't sure how I would deal with it again.

I thought about calling Peter and demanding he tell me what was going on, but I knew he would never give it up. Men never rat each other out. I thought about going there, and staking out the apartment from the Chinese restaurant across the street. I sat for a while, totally preoccupied by the sound of my own breathing and the otherwise silent apartment.

Sunday afternoon whizzed by. We hadn't met for brunch on Saturday and I was suffering from brunch withdrawal. What a cruel, cruel thing. Did he have brunch with her? I wondered. Did he take her to the diner on Second, or the little Italian place on Eightieth and Third? Or did they have brunch in bed? What if he was actually home screening his calls with Mali and laughing at me?

The thought didn't stop me from calling again and leaving a message.

"You there?" I said. "I think we should talk. Call me as soon as you get this."

I imagined their laughter.

Suddenly, I thought about calling Josh.

We hadn't spoken since that evening at my apartment. He hadn't been in class and I wasn't sure if his absences were work-related or kiss-related. I wanted to speak to him, but I didn't think calling him was the right move.

Because I felt vulnerable.

And the thing about feeling vulnerable is that you want to grab the nearest security blanket and take it to bed with you. And you want to be completely wrapped in it because it makes you feel protected and safe and warm.

It would have been too easy to call Josh and let him be that blanket.

By five in the evening John Paul still wasn't answering his phone.

Twelve

Peter was alone. He wasn't surprised to see me.

"Casey. Hey." He sounded tired and depressed. Cat Stevens was playing in the background.

"John Paul here?" I asked casually, trying my damnedest not to sound uptight. *It's all very cool,* my voice said.

Peter stared at me intently, trying to read me. He knew I was never this calm, even when I was completely relaxed.

"No," he said.

"Know where he is?"

"No." He shrugged. "I just woke up. I spent most of the night with Gabriella."

"You did?"

He left me at the door and walked back into the apartment. He picked up a joint from the table and lit it. He offered it to me.

I considered, said no.

"She had this last-minute thing to do in Boston or some-thing." He sat down on the sofa. "Did she mention that to you?"

"No." I closed the door and ventured inside. I sat next to him, aware that he was watching me, searching my face for a clue that I knew something. I wasn't in the mood to field questions about Gabriella's trip to Boston. "Really," I assured him. "No."

We were quiet for a minute, listening to Cat.

"I left him at Maddalena's," Peter offered.

"Alone?"

"I don't remember. I was pretty out of it."

I said, "You know Mali didn't go back to Gabriella's."

He held the joint out to me again. I kept my eyes fastened on his.

"She still isn't there," I added. "I stopped by before I came here."

"I don't know, Casey."

I stood up and started to pace the floor. He watched me.

"You're making me nervous," he said, standing up. "I'm going to go do my laundry."

"You aren't going to go out there and call him and tell him I'm here, are you?" I asked.

Peter gave me a look that said, *Have you gone off the deep end?*

"Help yourself to . . . whatever." He didn't answer the question. "I'll be in the laundry room if you need me."

He handed me the rest of his joint and left.

John Paul's bedroom door was open. I stared at it.

I know women who, left alone for thirty minutes in a man's apartment, can tell you his middle name, social security number, what his last three girlfriends looked like, who his last phone call was to, what he'd eaten for dinner the night before, and whether he'd eaten it alone.

I didn't have the stomach for that kind of detective work, but that didn't mean I was above taking a quick look. I took a few tokes from the joint, which was threatening to burn my fingertips, and continued to stare at the door to his room, mouthing the words to a Cat Stevens song I didn't even know I knew. I took the stairs two at a time. I went in.

The ironing board was still set up in the middle of the room, a half-ironed shirt rested on top of it. There was a pile of clothes on the floor, underneath the ironing board, and more clothes were hanging sloppily out of his drawers. But the bed was made like a bed in an army barracks. You could bounce a quarter on it. And the closet was still neat and uniform, like an obsession.

I checked for condom wrappers on the floor and under the furniture. There weren't any. At first I was relieved, but the relief wore off quickly. Where was he?

I sat on the bed and stared at the nightstand. I opened both drawers and searched them. There were the usual things you'd find in a nightstand: eyedrops, Vapo-Rub, Blistex, a small alarm clock. And there was something else. A strip of three golden, ribbed Avanti condoms.

Avanti? Golden? Ribbed?

We did not use colored, textured condoms. I was under the impression we liked simple. Extra thin. Trojans. And when we had a need for them, we didn't dabble in travel packs.

The Avanti condoms weren't dated, and there was no box. I couldn't check how old they were, or whether they had come in a pack of three, four, or six. I came to the conclusion that the only reason he would have them in his nightstand was because someone had given them to him.

I put the strip back in the drawer and closed it and I thought about the night before. How he'd called me, asked to come over, asked me not to hate him. Why not to hate him? I tried to remember if he'd sounded guilty. I started to seethe.

There weren't any condoms the first time. No phone call in the middle of the night asking if he could come over and keep me company. Just a late-night confession during a stupid moment of closeness in my apartment.

He said, "Do you ever think I might be the last person you sleep with?"

"Yes," I admitted immediately, knowing how strange it must have sounded. For a minute, I thought he was testing me. Nine months and already I thought he was the one. Nine months, and four years, I would have told him if he asked.

He said, "I think about it, too. A lot, lately."

I felt warm and nice after he said it. Partly from the margaritas we'd made in my kitchen, but mostly because those words felt so right.

He stood up. "Does it scare you?"

"No," I said. "It scares you?"

"Yes," he said. "Hell, yes."

He tried to change the subject, but I wouldn't let him. I insisted it was the right time to talk about things like what the next step should be and why he was thinking about not ever having sex with anyone else again. I said I didn't want any secrets. I said I could handle whatever he wanted to tell me.

"It only happened once," he began. "A month into our relationship, when we were still figuring it out. When we weren't sure."

I had always been sure.

"I wish I could take it back," he said.

And at that moment, in his room, over three months later, I was raging. Because the thing was, no one was giving me any points for playing by the rules.

People make you believe there's someone to turn to when something like this happens. But what happens when there isn't someone to turn to? When you already know what Ariadne and Dock are going to say and you know it isn't what you want to hear. When your mother and father don't know the whole story and you don't feel like explaining. When you don't believe in therapy.

The laundry room was in the basement of the building. Two small, semidark rooms—one for washing and one for drying—that always seemed to be empty. Peter was dozing in one of the chairs. I stared at him for a minute, at his chest rising and falling slowly with each breath. When he opened his eyes he looked directly at me.

"Hey," I said, my voice almost catching in my throat.

He stared at me, pushing his hands through his hair. He smiled, almost shyly, like he was embarrassed I'd caught him taking a nap.

"Hey," he said. "John Paul didn't show?"

"He didn't show."

He wiped the back of his hand over his mouth, leaned forward in a stretch. His muscles tugged subtly at the cotton. He looked at me and smiled again, and then he stood up. Instinctively I moved close to him. As though I needed his warmth and comfort.

I did.

He waited to see what I'd do, but I didn't do anything because I didn't want to be predictable.

I don't know if we were thinking the same thing. Maybe he thought he would just say something significant and send me on my way to figure it all out myself. He put his hands on my shoulders, looked me square in the eye, and said, "Sometimes people make mistakes."

I didn't know if he was talking about John Paul or me. I was just very aware of his hands on me. And it was strange, because he had touched me so many times before. But that moment, he felt different. He felt strong, like he could shield me from everything that hurt.

"Do you know something I should know?" I asked.

"I just know how it feels."

I sighed, shook my head. "You'll never know how it feels."

He stepped back and I could see something in his face had changed. He caught me letting my guard down.

"I know . . . " he began. "I know about feeling like nothing you do will ever bring you closer to the person you're in love with."

My body flushed as I imagined the sex John Paul and Mali had the night before—the sex that should have been mine—while I ingested five thousand calories' worth of pizza and played Solitaire on my laptop. I imagined the way they were huddled together at that moment, discussing how sad and celibate I was, discussing the best way to break the news to me. And I thought about Ariadne telling me to just fuck someone. Anyone. Not John Paul.

I took Peter's hand, moved it down to my waist and stopped, watched him. After a minute he squeezed me there, letting me know it was okay; he was in this. I reached up to touch his face. He leaned forward and we kissed, almost desperately, until he pulled away, covering my mouth with his hand.

"No," he said.

I moved backward, leaned against the wall. "I want this," I said.

"You want what?" His voice was soft. I could see he was trying to fight off a grin.

"This."

"Say it," he commanded, but I wouldn't.

And then he was standing near me, his mouth close to my ear, saying, "This?" Slipping his fingers inside my pants, inside my underwear. "This?" Peter so close to me, in me. "This?" I felt dazed for a second.

"Ow, shit," Peter said, catching himself on my zipper, pushing my pants down lower, fingers pressing against my skin, my thighs, my hips. "This?" Then pulling my hips closer, holding on to them, guiding them—for a second the image of John Paul entered my mind, then disappeared—moaning, licking, *licking,* fingers searching for my fingers, grasping them, tightening around them, pushing, deeper.

We leaned against the wall, spent. I felt tired, light-headed, overwhelmed. It had been so long. Three months doesn't seem like a long time, but it is, and I was glad my celibacy was over. I smiled to myself. Just one more thing I could cross off my Things to Do list.

Peter watched me. He took my smile as a sign that he was really good. He did have an ego. I pulled my pants up. He took my hand, stared at it, played with my fingers, and then he pulled me over to him and hugged me. I let him hold me for a while, the way I wanted John Paul to hold me and ignore my anger and not be afraid of my resistance. Gabriella had been lucky that way, to be with a guy who defied resistance.

Peter kissed me again and I let him because I wanted to be kissed again. I wanted to give him some more of my anger and hurt and I wanted to take some of his away. Because I did know part of him was hurting.

It was good for a minute. And then he whispered, "You were so tight. You were so good."

I did not move.

"That was your first time since . . . right?"

I stepped away from him as he tried to zip my pants back up for me. His hands were shaking and he was breathing hard. There was something about his shaking hands and his labored breathing. There was something about being so tight and so good. Suddenly, Peter summed up the reasons why I gave up sex in the first place. I'd imagined too many times John Paul doing and saying the same thing to Mali.

I zipped my pants up. I stared at the floor, felt him lean forward to kiss me again. I moved away.

"You're important to me," he said firmly.

"Oh, sure," I said, annoyed he would even go there. I can't count the number of times men have said I was important to them before and after we had sex. Sometimes it was a ploy to get me into bed. Other times it was a ploy to line up a second time.

"You've always been important to me," he claimed. "What do you think, something like this *just happens*?"

"Usually," I answered.

I stopped fidgeting with my pants and looked at him. He grinned, his eyebrows raised a little. Waiting. Waiting for what?

"What's up?" he said, pushing some hair out of my face.

"Nothing."

His sigh stopped short. Didn't want me to know what he was really thinking. That I was acting like a girlfriend. He remembered his clothes were still sitting in the washing machine. He snapped his fingers.

"Could have had these dry fifteen minutes ago," he said absently, pulling them out of the machine. He cursed when some dropped on the floor, looked at me as though I should help him. I didn't. Was I to be upgraded from quick-unexpected-lay to wife in two minutes?

"You mad at me?" he asked and I shook my head. "You wanna go for a drink or something? I'll pay. Least I can do."

Shit.

He stopped where he was. "Sorry," he said. "I didn't mean to sound . . . " He looked down at the wet clothes in his laundry basket. "Casey." His sometimes cold eyes glinted and I thought there was a hint of real sadness there.

"Forget it," I said.

I walked out of there and up the stairs to the lobby, where I spotted Polo, of all people, waiting for the elevator.

Talk about the coincidence from hell. What was *she* doing in John Paul's building? Dock lived two blocks away. It was the rare occasion when John Paul and I bumped into them in the neighborhood. But when we did we always said things like "So close, yet so far away." Stupid shit our parents used to say when they ran into friends who lived across the hall.

I thought about turning around and running back down to the basement or just making a quick getaway for the door. But just as I was going to make my escape I changed my mind. I had nothing to hide from her. She wasn't a *witness*.

She felt my presence before I even reached her, and when she saw me she didn't seem surprised.

"Hello," she said dully. "Funny meeting you here."

I smiled blandly. "What are you doing here?"

"Client."

"On a Sunday night?"

She looked at me, nodded. "Visiting John Paul?"

"Just came from there."

She looked behind me, at the staircase entrance I had just come out of. When the elevator door opened, Peter stepped out.

"I'm sorry. I didn't mean any of that shit I said. You can't just leave like—" He saw Polo and stopped midsentence. "Hi," he said awkwardly.

"Hello, Peter." She walked inside the elevator.

Peter stood in the door, holding it open, frowning at me. "You coming up?" he asked.

I shook my head, looking at Polo. She was staring straight ahead. Her face was expressionless.

"I just came from there," I muttered.

He stared at me hard, waited.

"Would you let the door go?" Polo asked.

Peter glanced at her, then back at me. "Come up," he whispered.

I refused. He let the elevator door close.

Thirteen

I waited for the next elevator. Really, there was nowhere else I wanted to go. I didn't want to go home. No one was there to tell this thing to. And didn't I want to say, "Shit, what was *she* doing there?" to someone? Anyone. Peter.

In the hallway Peter was just unlocking the door to the apartment. He watched me blankly, held the door open for me. Inside, we didn't say a word. He dropped the keys on the sofa, picked up an ashtray, a lighter and a pack of cigarettes from the table. He started to head up the stairs.

"Peter?"

I wanted him to sit at the table with me and gossip about how easy it had been. I wanted to say it out loud so that it wouldn't feel like I was keeping a secret.

He stopped, turned slightly, waited. The smile on his face stopped me from saying anything. He thought I wanted him again. He thought I had come back for more.

When I didn't say anything he started up the stairs again and went inside his room. He left the door open like an invitation.

I called my apartment, checked my messages, decided there was no excuse I would accept from my boyfriend anymore. I stared at Peter's door for a minute, and then I left.

I went home, showered, ate something. I still didn't want to sit in my apartment with my telephone and answering machine that held no messages from John Paul, but I didn't have a huge choice. Where was I going to go?

I started to wonder why I thought I needed him so much, and I didn't want to wonder about that. What if it had been John Paul standing in that lobby instead of Polo? What if it had been Gabriella?

It didn't matter that, technically, she wasn't his girlfriend anymore and that he was single. With friends, you had to give it six months to a year, and even then, it was tricky. I knew that no matter how broken up they were, they would always have a strong bond. He would always be *the* boyfriend for her. And was I thinking about Peter and Gabriella, or John Paul and Mali? I wondered.

Sometimes in movies, a man falls in love with a woman while his girlfriend is standing right next to him at a party. It's maddening how this man and woman make eye contact and fall in love while his girlfriend is looking at something else. I often wondered if there was a moment like that in my life. Was I standing next to John Paul the moment he and Mali shared that look? It never crossed my mind that it could have been the other way around. Was she standing next to him when he realized he could love me?

It also bothered me when I thought about those moments happening between Peter and me. I couldn't recall them, but they had to have been there. The moments when we laughed at something that was just so real for us, but no one else in the room got it. The moments when he put his hand on my arm, kept it there, and moved it away only when Gabriella looked in our direction.

Shit. I felt emotional and lost and alone. I wanted to call my mother in California, but I never called L.A. And more likely than not, Mom and Dad were out with their film and television friends.

And I wouldn't know where to begin. I would have to explain that I'd been celibate because John Paul cheated on me and I'd just ended my celibacy with Gabriella's ex-boyfriend seconds after she dumped him. I'd have to explain that I'd made the move from punishment celibacy to revenge sex in less than five months. Mom would lose sleep knowing her daughter was cheesier than the soap opera she was in.

So, I did not call my mother. And I forced myself not to call John Paul again.

The doorbell rang a few hours after I came home. I was lying on my sofa, half sleeping. I ignored it. I didn't want company. After a minute, I heard a set of keys rattling. My front door opened.

"Don't turn on the light," I warned.

"Why didn't you let me in?" he asked.

"Why didn't you call? Why didn't you come earlier?"

"I did call," he said solemnly.

"In the middle of the night. I was sleeping. Was she with you then?"

He turned on the light. I shielded my eyes until they ad-

justed. I wanted to check him for evidence of her. He should
have been thinking the same thing about me.

He looked down at the keys in his hands. I looked at them
too. Was he going to give them back to me? Was that how he
was going to do this?

"I know I should have come sooner. But I needed time to
think."

I sat up, rubbed at my eyes, tried to get it together. He stuck
the keys in his coat pocket and, sickeningly enough, I was relieved. Then he took off his coat and flung it on the nearest
chair.

"I missed her," he said. "I didn't want to have to explain that
to you, or make you feel better about it. I didn't feel I needed
your permission. I just wanted to talk to a friend."

"How nice for you," I snapped. "You just wanted to talk to a
friend. Did it cross your mind that talking to your friend all
night might seem like you were fucking her?"

"No," he said calmly. "Not if you trust me."

"I do trust you. As much as you should trust me."

He hesitated. "What does that mean?"

"Figure it out."

He frowned, but he didn't try to figure it out. He took a pack
of cigarettes from his back pocket, pulled one out, and stared
at it.

"You don't know everything," he said after a while.

I turned away as my breath caught in my chest. I didn't
know if I wanted to know everything now that he was willing
to tell it. I was sure I knew what had happened between them,
but suddenly I wasn't sure I wanted it confirmed.

"Listen to me," he said earnestly. "You don't know things."

"You keep saying that."

"We were close," he said. "But we aren't close anymore. And there were things we went through together that I can't get into."

I looked at him again. "You should get into them." My voice was soft, steady, firm.

"When we were together," he began slowly, "she was supposed to do this MFA program for dance. But she was going through this thing with her mother. There was another baby and Mali had to be around to help. She gave up the program, which triggered a depression. You know, the chances you let slip through your fingers . . . shit." He shook his head. "I want you to understand this, but it's not easy to explain. She gave up her life to help someone who messed up theirs."

"Her mother," I said.

"Exactly."

"So she's bitter."

"She made a choice to give up her career and stay here."

"Okay," I said. "But that was years ago. What does it have to do with you?"

"It was a very bad depression, Casey. And it was a very tough time for her. Us. We were young. And to be honest, our relationship was debilitating."

"Then why did you stay with her?"

He thought about his answer carefully. "I was just starting out in advertising. She was my support system and I was hers. We went through a lot together. And I can't just turn my back on her now, no matter how much you want me to. I can't. But that's all it is. Sometimes she needs me."

Men want love all of their lives, and when it comes they push it away and say they're confused. But need is a different story. Need, they can handle. Mali *needed* him. That was all she had to do. And it wasn't that I was insensitive and didn't find the tale of Mali's missed opportunities heartbreaking. It was just that, well, *I* was his girlfriend. What was I supposed to do during those all-important moments when he couldn't turn his back on her and comforted her with a quick romp in the sack? Find more solace with Peter?

That's when I decided to tell him. It wasn't about revenge or rubbing anyone's face in my triumphant battle over celibacy. It was about *my needs* and waking him up from this Mali-needs-me-and-I-need-to-be-there illusion. I was not going to lose to some depressed chick who couldn't face life because she couldn't *dance*.

I opened my mouth to say it, and then I closed it again. I wanted it to come out the way it should come out.

"Casey," he said before I could get it out. "I haven't touched her ever since that time. It was one time."

"What?" I couldn't have heard that right.

"We just talked."

That was good news, wasn't it? Great news, in fact. But why wasn't I smiling? Why was I trying to find a snag in this information? I didn't want it to be true the same way I didn't want it to be true the first time he'd told me he slept with her. Because what the hell was I supposed to do with my anger?

"Then where were you last night? Today? Why didn't Mali go back to Gabriella's?"

"How do you know she didn't go back to Gabriella's?"

"Gabriella told me."

He shrugged, stared off in the distance. "I don't know."

"I called you this afternoon."

He looked at me. "I slept late, turned off the phone."

"I went to see you."

"I was here. In Brooklyn. Looking for you."

"Where is she?"

"I don't know."

"You expect me to believe you turned off your phone?"

He nodded, eyes narrowing. "You told me to leave last night. You hung up on me. Now you want to condemn me for turning off my phone?"

I took a deep breath.

"How much more of this do you want me to take?" he asked. "You want to own me?"

"I don't want to own you," I said. "Or tell you what to do. But you loved her. And when she's around things are different. There's a certain way you make me feel . . . insignificant. And I don't know what to do when I feel that way."

"I didn't fuck her," he said. "I've always been straight with you about my feelings. I made a mistake once and I told you. Don't I get credit for that?"

I imagined what Ariadne would say. No doubt it would be something funny and concise, something that would leave him speechless and stupid. Then she would turn to me and say people don't treat you like shit unless you give off that vibe that you want to be shit. They go where you tell them to.

"We are different when we're with her," I insisted.

He stared at me for a long time, trying to figure out why I wouldn't let all of these feelings go and just accept his truth.

"What's wrong with you?" He shook his head. "I . . . you know what? If I slept with her, I would have told you. You would have been the first to know."

"Mali would have been the first to know."

He opened his mouth, and then he closed it and bit his lip. He bolted out of the apartment so fast I couldn't stop him. And I didn't feel good at all.

I was no Ariadne: grounded and strong and untouchable. Sometimes, Ariadne was no Ariadne. She was the one who wrote love poems when she fell in love, and angry letters when she was dumped. She was the one in therapy. And maybe Larry was working for her. There were those moments when you just needed that man with the degree in listening to be there for you. But Larry didn't have all the answers. He couldn't tell me what to do next.

Fourteen

When class was over on Monday, I sat in my office and tried to concentrate on a schedule for the next semester. But I really wanted to call John Paul and rehash what we'd said to each other before he took off the night before. I wanted to get it all straight.

I picked up the telephone. I was going to patch things up with my boyfriend. I was going to get my life back on track. I was inspired.

"Casey?"

The woman in the doorway was young, about nineteen. She walked into the office and dropped into the chair next to my desk. I felt an immediate dislike for her.

"I'm worried about my future," she said.

"Who are you?"

"I'm *Terry.*" She sounded offended. "I'm in your Introduction to Cinema class on Tuesdays."

"Oh. Now I remember you," I lied.

"I *really* need someone to talk to," she said, staring straight ahead.

I stared at the girl like she was crazy. Why would she choose me as the professor to come to?

"Is this related to school?" I asked coldly.

"Yes." She rolled her eyes heavenward, which made me want to kick her. "I'm worried about my future."

"Okay. Maybe I can help," I said, knowing perfectly well I couldn't. I was worried about *my* future. At least she was nineteen.

"I'm going to be a junior in September," she began. "And I feel like I haven't learned anything. I feel like—and this has nothing to do with you—all of the professors are settled in this teaching thing and could give a rat's ass whether or not I become a filmmaker. It's really depressing. When my professors, the people I'm supposed to look up to, have no desire to make it in the business, where does that leave me? I don't want to end up teaching when I graduate. Because how much of a failure would that make me? I bet this isn't what you set out to do with your life."

"Terry," I said. "If you're so unhappy, why don't you leave?"

"Excuse me?"

"Leave," I repeated. "Drop out. Why stay here if you're not getting what you want?"

Terry stood up. She looked completely insulted. "You know what? Now I understand why you teach. You probably can't do anything else."

She turned on her heel and headed out. When I was sure she wouldn't look back, I gave her the finger.

Actually, I had my doubts that any professor cared whether or not his students became anything once they were out of the classroom. I know I didn't. I know none of my former professors cared what became of me. And I wasn't in the mood to dole out advice.

Terry was right. It *was* depressing.

But I didn't care about Terry. I didn't care if she ended up being the next Steven Spielberg, or if she ended up managing a McDonald's in Bayside, Queens. (Though I would have preferred she end up with the Bayside gig.) I just didn't want her to remember me. I didn't want her to find herself with some young man one night, a man who had the whole world in front of him, telling him that Professor Beck steered her in the wrong direction. I couldn't even live with the *thought* of that.

My inspiration to get my life back on track was sucked out of me like a vacuum. I left my office and ended up in Ariadne's. She was sitting at her desk, reading and smoking a cigarillo. I sat down and stared out the window.

"I'm giving up feminism," I said.

"*Hello.*" She didn't even look up. "You never were a feminist."

"Yes," I said. "Some parts of me were. I had feminist views."

She closed the book she was reading and took off her glasses.

"In this world that you have created where you're a feminist," she began, "what incident has made you decide to give it up?"

Okay, so I'd never actually been a feminist. But there were signs that I could have been. I believed women had an obligation to one another. I never dated men my friends liked. I read Gloria Steinem. In high school. So, *The View* made me want to lose my lunch, but that was because it did more harm to the image of four women in the same room than it did good. And I was cynical about movies that insinuated friendships between women were major support systems, like telephone lines running across America. And I had this one indiscretion with Peter.

But I believed women had an obligation to one another. That was enough. Right?

Ariadne tapped her pen on her desk, waiting for my answer. I picked up her cigarillo from the ashtray, watched it burn, and debated whether or not I wanted to smoke it. She stared at me. She knew I hated cigarillos.

I stuck it in my mouth.

"Okay," she said, grabbing the cigarillo and putting it back in the ashtray. "What the hell is going on?"

I put the words I wanted to say in the order they should come out of my mouth. Then I looked at her, really looked at her, and told her the truth.

"I went to see John Paul yesterday."

"And?"

"He wasn't home; Peter was. And when he left to do his laundry I went through John Paul's things and I found these condoms. . . ." My voice trailed off. The condoms. I hadn't asked John Paul to explain the condoms.

"Go on," Ariadne said.

"I fucked him," I blurted. "I fucked Peter."

I watched her face as my words sunk in. Her mouth dropped open slowly. She put the book she'd been reading on the desk, and then she stood up and closed her office door.

"*What?*"

"Right there in the laundry room," I groaned.

"Get the fuck out of here," she said, unbelieving.

I desperately explained my situation. That's what you do after you've just been insulted by a nineteen-year-old who has her whole life ahead of her, and the twenty-minute walk around the school has helped you come up with this conclusion: you're a loser and a failure.

Ariadne sat down. "So that's why you didn't show up at Bobo's. Dock and I were waiting for you."

"Oh God." I covered my eyes.

"It's not the end of the world," she soothed. "And it means all of that celibacy crap is finished with, right?"

I nodded.

"Why didn't you call me yesterday?" she asked.

"I didn't want to tell anyone. It's not like winning a spelling bee."

She grinned.

"I fucked Peter. I don't think it's funny."

"I know." She stopped grinning.

"I'm a failure," I said. "I failed John Paul *and* Gabriella."

"First of all, stop feeling sorry for yourself," she scolded. "Peter and Gabriella aren't together anymore. And to hell with John Paul. This wouldn't be happening if it weren't for that asshole. It was okay for him to go out there and pump a few more bullets into that slut, right?"

"Well . . ."

She narrowed her eyes at me.

I said, "I don't think anything happened."

She sucked her teeth. "When I called you yesterday, Mali had been out all night with John Paul. Now you're telling me nothing happened? Is that what he told you?"

"He said they talked."

"He's lying," she said matter-of-factly.

"I've been through it a hundred times and I know you hate him, but I love him and I have to believe him. He isn't worth fighting for if I'm not willing to believe him."

She watched me for a long time. I wanted her to say something profound, the way the best friend is supposed to, but I understood if she couldn't.

"Okay" was all she said.

"Now I'm left with this *thing*. With Peter. And I keep thinking about why I needed to do it."

"You needed affection," she told me. "That's what it all boils down to. Celibacy isn't healthy. You've been denying yourself a very necessary aspect of social life for a long time. You can tell yourself that it's how things should be, but your body knows better. The sex was there, offered to you, and you took it. It's very basic. Being horny, and sexually attracted to a handsome man you have a decent rapport with, is not a bad thing. And that's not about being a woman. It's about being human. You made a mistake because the man in your life really scarred you, and now it's his turn to forgive."

Ariadne always made things sound so logical. I could have told myself she was right. Horniness, attraction, decent rapport all sounded good to me. And it would get me off the hook, to boot.

"I don't know if I buy that," I said. "I mean, they sell us on this idea of sisterhood and feminism and we buy it because we're supposed to. We think we have this automatic bond with someone because we're women. We think the real battle of the sexes is with men."

"So what are you saying? You shouldn't have slept with Peter because you're a woman?"

"Ariadne . . . "

She said, "It's natural to be tempted by other people even if they *belong* to someone else. Someone close to you."

"But what are you meant to do about it?"

"You're meant to make the mistakes people make, and

you're meant to learn from them. You're meant to do what it takes to make yourself happy. You aren't meant to make up stupid excuses and theories and give up on feminism. You never were a feminist. And even if you were, it doesn't make your thing with Peter a crime."

"Would you be saying that if it were your boyfriend I slept with?"

"It wouldn't be my boyfriend," she shot back. "I wouldn't be with a man who would seduce my friend."

"What if *I* did the seducing?"

"This is why you aren't a feminist." She was annoyed. "You're always defending men. You still think they need defending. Since when has a man defended you?"

I wasn't trying to make a point about chivalry and whether a man had defended my honor in the last year and a half. I was trying to come clean to the one person I knew would love me no matter what I told her. I was trying to admit that *I* left John Paul's apartment in search of Peter in the basement of their building. *I* wanted Peter to reach out and touch me. Because there was something between us. I didn't make that up. It was something we ignored because we had Gabriella and John Paul in common.

Ariadne picked up her cigarillo, which was quickly burning down to a nub.

"The next time you see John Paul," she said, "sleep with him."

I stood up.

"Okay," she said calmly, cigarillo in the corner of her mouth. "Whatever you're feeling now is what you're supposed to be feeling. I'm sorry I said anything. I'm going to let you handle it."

Sometimes it's okay to hate your best friend. I started to leave.

"Don't be that woman." Her voice was soft. "The woman who settled."

I turned to look at her again. "You think I'm settling?"

"I think you're settling."

"I really love John Paul."

She took the cigarillo from her mouth. "Has it ever crossed your mind that maybe you don't love him? Maybe you don't want him?"

"No," I said. "It never crossed my mind."

She didn't look convinced. "Would it be so terrible not to love this guy? I mean, are you willing to let him be the reason why you don't get the things in life you really want?"

I didn't say anything.

"Why is he so much?" she asked. "What does he do? Does the fucking world make sense when you're with him?"

"No." I could feel my blood pressure rise. "He's just there. I feel safe with him. People treat me differently when I'm with him. They treat me better. Is that okay with you?"

Ariadne nodded, sorry for me.

"Sometimes it gets lonely," I continued. "It's the kind of lonely you and Dock can't cure. I don't want to feel that loneliness the rest of my life. And I hate it that Mali can just show up and try to take everything away from me."

"Your problem has always been that you think this is about you and Mali. It isn't. It's about you and John Paul."

"It is about me and Mali. She's trying to take something that's mine."

Ariadne grabbed my hand and pulled me closer to her. "Some women stay with a certain guy because they know he's a good thing and they'd be crazy to let a good thing go, to let some undeserving bitch get her hands on him. But some good things aren't good for *you*. Who cares about being lonely for a couple of years when it means you're free to find the right thing." She touched my hand to her cheek. "We've known each other for a long time. I love you. I don't want you to hurt."

I nodded, unable to look at her. "Why does she still mean so much to him?"

"First love, maybe. First sex. They say you never forget your first love or your first sex." She sighed. "I did."

"John Paul was my first love."

"What a shame." She pushed some hair out of my face and smiled. "You okay?"

"I have a class," I said. "We'll talk later?"

I left Ariadne feeling agitated, and I started to think about my feelings. I was that girl I always felt sorry for in movies, the girl in second place, the insignificant other. And I didn't want to be that. His second love. His insignificant other.

I was about to be thirty. Thirty. And what did I have? I had the drama with John Paul and Mali and Peter. And I had a job I hated. I had to start looking for the thing that made me happy. I didn't want to be a depressed thirty-year-old with pent-up rage because I didn't own a home, or I was married to the wrong person and hated my kids.

I decided I needed a second opinion. An opinion I wanted to hear. I thought I could get it from Dock, even though I wasn't sure what it would be.

He was sitting at the bar at Bobo's, writing out the evening's specials on a chalkboard. I waved at Johnny and sat next to him.

"You almost missed me," he said. "I'm off in ten minutes."

"Do you want to have dinner?"

"Can't." He lifted the chalkboard and stared at his work.

Then he held it up to me. I gave him a thumbs-up approval. "I'm meeting Polo for dinner downtown. I'll take the train with you, though."

I nodded, disappointed.

"Polo told me she saw you last night," he said casually.

"Oh." My voice was guarded. "Is that all she told you?"

"No," he said slowly, giving me a sidelong glance.

"What else did she tell you?"

"That you weren't alone."

"I wasn't alone."

"No." He handed the chalkboard to Johnny and stood up. Then he grabbed his jacket from behind the bar and motioned he was ready to leave.

Outside, he looped his arm through mine as we walked to the train together.

"She didn't suspect anything. She just thought you and Peter were—"

"What?"

"Agitated."

I stared at the ground while we walked.

"But you knew," I said. "I don't have to tell you."

He nodded. "And I understand."

It freaked me out that my best friends understood what had happened.

"So, what are you going to do?" he asked.

"Well, I'm not going to tell Gabriella."

"You aren't?"

"No. Definitely not. No one really wants to know the absolute truth."

He nodded, agreeing.

"And I think telling her would do more harm than good."

"You don't have to convince me," he said.

"Part of me wants to tell John Paul. He should know I lost my celibacy."

Dock cracked a smile.

"But I don't want it to seem like revenge," I added.

"Wasn't it?"

"Not completely." I shook my head. "I don't know. Wouldn't you want Polo to tell you if she was unfaithful?"

"No," he said curtly.

"I don't believe that. I don't believe you wouldn't want to know."

He stopped walking and faced me. "You should let it go."

"'Let it go.' I hate when people say that. It's like saying you should stop eating if you want to lose weight."

"Sorry." He shook his head. "It is a stupid thing to say." He stared at a car driving past. Then he looked at me. "I wouldn't want to know."

"Why not?"

"Because." He sighed. "Don't hurt me because you fucked up, you know? Because you feel guilty. You live with it. Don't bring it to me. Because after you tell me, I'll always see you differently. That will never change."

He looked down at the ground and I wondered if there was something happening in his life that he wasn't telling me. Was there something more to Polo's Sunday night visit to a client in John Paul's building? He gently tugged at my arm and we started walking again. "What are you thinking?"

I said, "I wonder why he told me about Mali the first time."

"I've wondered."

"You have?"

Dock nodded. "I bet he wouldn't have told you if he knew he'd have to go without sex for six months."

"I bet you're right," I said darkly.

On the train we sat across from an attractive woman. I felt her eyes on us, so I focused on the floor. When the train stopped, she stood up and got off.

Dock laughed. "Thank you for getting on the train," he said as she passed the window. "Thank you for smiling at me and being alive."

"She smiled?"

"Yes."

"How?"

"What do you mean? She turned back to look at me before she got off and smiled."

"Did she show teeth?"

"No," he said. "Why?"

"What if we were together?" I asked. "What if we were in love, or married? Why would she flirt with you?"

"Because she knew I couldn't pursue it." He shook his head. "She wasn't flirting. She was flattered. She was thanking me for admiring her."

I didn't believe him.

"Seriously," he insisted. "*I* was flirting with *her*. Blame me."

"Still, why would she flirt with a man who flirts with her in front of his girlfriend? He's obviously a sleaze."

Dock turned away from me and stared out the window. He was probably thinking of all the times he made passes at women while Polo's head was turned.

"Have you ever cheated on her?" I whispered.

He didn't answer.

As we pulled into the next station he looked at me. "Listen," he said. "I don't know what's going on with John Paul or Mali. That's something you have to ask them. But I do know one thing you can't deny."

"What?"

"He chose you. Every day after it happened, after you told him you didn't want him to touch you, after you punished him, he chose you."

"Then why didn't he call?" I asked.

Dock stared at me for a long time and I waited for this answer he was preparing to give me. This answer I hoped would make it all make sense.

"Because he's a guy."

The train pulled into West Fourth and I got off to transfer to the F train. Dock waved at me from the window and blew me a kiss.

Across the tracks, on the uptown platform, I spotted Josh with a woman. He looked up, but I turned away before he could see me. Then the uptown train pulled in. When it pulled out, the platform was empty.

Fifteen

The next day I saw Josh in school. He was talking to a man I didn't recognize. I thought about turning around and walking in the opposite direction. But something stopped me. I didn't want to run away from him.

"Hey," he said as I walked past him. His friend slapped him on the back and headed down the hall. "Where are you headed?"

"Home."

He nodded, looked around. "I'll take the train with you."

We walked to the train in silence. A few students waved at us as they passed.

"You haven't been in class," I said once we reached the station. My throat felt scratchy. I was hoping he didn't notice the goose bumps that were popping up on my skin.

"You should have said hi," he said.

"I didn't see you."

He shook his head. "On the platform yesterday. We were on opposite sides of the track. I was with Priscilla."

Priscilla?

"I saw you," he admitted.

"Then *you* should have said hello."

Suddenly, he looked painfully serious. "I didn't say hello because I didn't want you to see me with her. Then I realized you must have seen me with her. You were looking right at us."

"Is she in one of my classes?" I asked stupidly.

He shook his head. "She's Priscilla. We used to go together. Remember I mentioned her? Four years . . . "

"The ex-girlfriend." I nodded, remembering.

I was relieved when I saw the train pulling in. I wanted to be away from him. I didn't want to deal with the signals my body was sending me. "It was good to see you," I said as I moved toward the train. For some reason, I didn't think he would get on.

Inside, he stood close to me.

"When I first met you," he said, "I thought about you constantly."

I swallowed hard. You can't have this, I reminded myself. It doesn't matter that your heart has sped up and you're having trouble breathing, and he's staring at you so sincerely, the way no one has ever stared at you before. You know it's too good to be true.

"You live in Brooklyn?" I asked, even though I knew he did. I remembered. My voice was hoarse.

He ignored my question.

"Was the other night about getting back at John Paul?" he asked.

I knew he meant the kiss and I knew I should tell him the truth.

"No," I said casually. "Was it about getting back at Priscilla?"

"No." He started to smile.

"Was it about getting an A in my class?"

The smile was lost. "Is that what you think?"

No, it wasn't what I thought.

"I don't give a shit about my grade in that class. You know that. Fail me. The kiss was about you."

"If you want to call it a kiss," I said cruelly.

"Why are you afraid of me?" he asked. "I don't want to hurt you."

"We do a lot of things we don't want to do," I told him.

"I *won't* hurt you."

I stared at my shoes.

"Would you have dinner with me?"

"I can't."

"I won't ask again," he warned.

I looked at him, finally. "Then I won't have to say no again."

He opened his mouth to say something, but no words came out. He looked away from me, at the other people on the train. He parted his lips again, but still no words left them, just a short laugh. He avoided looking at me. His face was going red, and he was genuinely hurt.

I wished I could take back what I said.

He checked to see which station we were pulling into. The train stopped and he didn't turn around to say good-bye when he got off.

John Paul was leaning against the front door of Maddalena's, smoking a cigarette. We hadn't seen each other since Sunday.

"I'm glad you called," he said.

We sat at a booth in back.

He said, "I got a commercial."

I looked at him, smiled. "That's fantastic. The peanut guys?"

He nodded. "Yeah. Believe it or not. I'll be working late the next few months, but it's worth it. I have a good team."

"I'm happy for you."

"I knew you would be."

I stared at the menu. He stared at his cigarette.

"We should talk," I said, closing the menu.

He looked at me earnestly. "Sometimes I really need you."

"Sometimes I need you, too."

"What the hell is happening to us, then?"

I wanted to tell him everything, from what I had planned the night Mali arrived to what happened with Peter. But the bartender stopped by the table and John Paul ordered two margaritas.

"It's hard to tell you things" was all I could say once the bartender left.

"Tell me everything," he pleaded.

I couldn't and he didn't push. We sat silently until the margaritas arrived. We let them sit.

"Why did you tell me?" I asked. "That first time. About you and Mali."

He straightened and rubbed his temples. Then he frowned. "I don't know."

I rested my head on the wall behind me and stared at the door. "Were you sure I'd forgive you?"

He lifted his head but I didn't check if he was looking at me.

I said, "Or were you hoping I'd leave?"

"Nothing happened." His voice was quiet and sad. "You have to believe me."

Finally, I looked at him. "I believe you. But that isn't what I asked."

He took my hand and squeezed it. "I miss you."

"I know," I said. "But you still haven't answered my question."

He let go of my hand.

"I don't know." He sounded frustrated. "You want me to say I regret telling you? I regret that you won't let me touch you. I regret . . . "

"I let you touch me," I said. "I've been trying to get things back on track. But every time we get together . . . "

The door opened and Mali walked in.

" . . . she walks in."

"Hello," Mali said. I hadn't seen her since Saturday night. She looked the same. I don't know why I expected her to look different. She stared at John Paul dully, but he refused to look at her. We didn't invite her to sit with us, and she didn't take it upon herself to sit next to him like she usually did.

"How are you, Paulie boy?" she asked.

He didn't answer right away. Finally, he looked at her. He said, "Fine, thanks."

There was a minute of silence and I broke it. "Do you want to go?" I asked him.

John Paul pulled his eyes away from Mali long enough to look at me. I hated the feeling I had in the pit of my stomach. I didn't want to think about what it meant. I didn't want to consider the thought that was deep in the back of my mind. I didn't want to consider that I couldn't believe him.

"Yeah," he said.

The bartender stopped by to see how we were doing. Mali ordered a whiskey sour and John Paul asked for the check.

"Take care," she said to him, and then she found her own table.

John Paul shook his head. His eyes were glistening. He

looked young and a little scared. "It's weird to be around her. You want to get out of here?"

"Why is it weird?" I asked.

"You know," he said. "This whole thing."

"But nothing happened," I said stiffly. "Why would it be weird?"

"You know what I mean."

The bartender arrived with our check. John Paul paid and we left.

Outside, he put his arm around my shoulders. I tensed. His arm felt awkward and heavy. I didn't feel the goose bumps I felt when I was with Josh.

"I don't know what you meant," I said.

"Well, I told her I didn't want her, would never want her. I told her she should have never come back."

I stopped walking. "Why did you have to tell her that? If you were talking about her mother, and you were helping her get through this *depression,* why did you have to tell her that? How did it come up?"

He frowned. "I thought I explained that to you."

"No." I shook my head. "You said she needed you. Sometimes she needs you."

"She wanted to know if there was any way we could get back together. I thought I told you that."

"You didn't." I felt my heartbeat quicken.

"She accepted it when I told her no. But . . . you saw her. She's not happy."

I stared at the ground, thought about it. "Disappointed. Is that all?"

"No," he said, forcing me to look up at him. "It took me a long time to admit it to myself, and I was a jerk about it. But I love you. And it's all that I'm doing. It's all that I want to do. She knows that. She sees it."

I wasn't convinced.

"*I love you.* I'm going to prove that to you."

I stepped back. "I love you, too," I said quietly. But, really, I was unsure.

I had my head down on my desk and I was starting to take a nap when there was a knock on the door. I groaned, assuming it was one of my students.

"Beck," the voice said sternly.

I looked into the face of Professor Walker, a snob who taught the most coveted courses in the department: Screen Directing and Cinematography.

"There's a call that came in for you on my phone line," he informed me. "Would you like to take it?"

He stared at me like I was a homeless person who smelled bad. I thought his attitude toward me was unfair. After all, I was the one who caught him with that student in the editing room and I never told Zabrowski. But Professor Walker didn't thank me, or bother to say hello when we passed in the halls. He pretended not to fear what I knew, though I could tell by the way he stared at me from the corner of his eye that he did.

"Thanks." I stood up and walked past him. His office was next door.

"Just me," Gabriella said cheerfully.

"Oh." I was taken by surprise. "Hello."

"'Oh. Hello.' What kind of greeting is that?"

"I thought you were out of town."

She said, "I was. I'm back now."

"How's your grandmother?"

"Good. Good. How are you?"

"Okay."

"So I hear. This thing with Mali worked out."

"If you want to call it that. Who told you?"

"A little bird told me. He sat on my shoulder and said everything's okay with your best friend."

I tried to laugh, but it wasn't funny. Since when was I her best friend?

"I'm glad I was wrong," she said.

"That was a quick trip. I thought you were staying longer."

"Please," she said. "I spent enough time with Granny. Oh, and I've decided to have a big party for Peter's birthday."

"Really? I thought you and Peter were—"

"It's all forgotten," she informed me. "We got back together last night. He had tons of flowers waiting for me when I got in."

I held my breath, confused about how I should feel.

"Are you there?"

"When you called me . . . " I began.

"I was a mess. Forget it."

"I can't forget it. Did you really go to Boston to see your grandmother?"

She hesitated, and then she said, "Of course. Why else would I go to Boston?"

"I don't know," I said. "I just wondered if . . . "

"What?"

"Nothing. I'm glad you and Peter are together again."

She made a funny noise. "I wasn't sure. I thought it was over for good this time. But I was out there, in Boston, watching Granny, and she's just *so old*. Old and lonely. And she doesn't smell so hot, you know? And I realized a lot of things. Like how much I love him."

"Oh God." It came out like I was being strangled. "That's beautiful."

"It worked out for all of us, didn't it?" she said.

"You bet."

"And the other good news is that Mali is actually planning to leave. Did you know that? She got in touch with that friend in Brooklyn. She quit the café."

I took a deep breath. "When?"

"Oh, I don't know," she said. "While I was away. She was an awful waitress. Let's get together. Why don't you help me plan Peter's party?"

Professor Walker stood in the doorway, trying to intimidate me with his glare. I turned my back to him.

"Plan it?"

"We can figure out a theme and what kind of food to serve."

I sighed, feeling self-conscious under Professor Walker's evil eye. "I'm just really busy."

"I need five minutes," she persisted.

I hesitated.

"Please. It's a good excuse to get together. And talk."

"Okay," I gave in. "Sure."

Professor Walker cleared his throat and finally stepped inside his office. He stood close to me, straightening some papers on his desk, indicating I had overstayed my welcome. I motioned to let him know I'd be off the phone in a minute.

"I have to go," I said a little unsteadily.

"I'll call you," she said.

Sixteen

That Thursday I found myself in front of the little café where Gabriella worked. It was a conscious decision, of course. I couldn't say I just happened to be in the neighborhood. The café was in Greenwich Village, miles away from my apartment, and school was on the Upper East Side.

I stopped in the doorway when I saw Peter sitting at a table, reading a book. I turned to leave, but the annoying chimes on the door alerted everyone that I was there. Peter looked up.

"This is a surprise," Gabriella said, walking over to give me a hug. She made a big fuss about the fact that I never visited her at work. I said something silly, like "You change jobs so frequently," which was true, and she laughed. She pulled out the empty chair across from Peter and commanded me to sit.

Peter closed the book he was reading and stared at me.

"What can I get you?" Gabriella asked. "Peter's drinking a cappuccino. You want cappuccino? Are you hungry?"

"Okay," I said.

She frowned at me. "Okay, what?"

"I'll have something simple."

"Did you eat dinner yet?" Peter asked. "Or were you plan-ning to have dinner here? With Gabriella?"

I hadn't eaten dinner. I had planned to ask Gabriella if she wanted to grab a bite to eat with me so we could talk. "I ate something earlier. I'll just have a slice of cake."

Gabriella winked at me. "Good choice."

"Hey," Peter said once she left.

I couldn't look him in the eye. I picked up the book he was reading. "*War and Peace*. How is it?"

"I'm reading the war parts. They're okay."

Gabriella brought over a slice of carrot cake. One of my fa-vorites. I smiled my thanks. She was about to say something when a group of people walked in. She greeted them.

"Why are you here?" Peter asked.

"Visiting."

"Bullshit," he said softly. "You never visit her at work."

"I'm usually busy."

He pulled his chair closer to the table. "Do you remember what you were like when John Paul told you about Mali?"

"Of course I do," I said.

The day after John Paul told me about Mali, Peter and Gabriella came to my apartment and slept in my parents' bed. I woke to Peter making an enormous breakfast for the three of us. And while Gabriella slept late, Peter and I silently ate pancakes and sausages. And when I started to cry unexpect-edly, he put his arms around me and told me it would be okay. I cried on his shoulder that morning. He pulled up his T-shirt and wiped away my tears. He said, "Mistakes are never easy."

"Now imagine if Mali told you because she wanted to *get it off her chest.*"

"How do you know I'm here to get something off my chest?" I asked.

"Because I know you." He spoke through clenched teeth. "I *know* you."

The chimes on the front door tinkled and I looked up to see John Paul walking in. For a second, time stopped. He was there, without me. It was weird to know John Paul was doing something I didn't know he did. How often did he meet Peter at the cafés Gabriella worked in?

Gabriella came over to give John Paul a kiss. "Peter said Casey was busy," she told him.

"He did?" I looked at Peter. *What were you planning?* my look said.

Gabriella mussed Peter's hair. "Silly rabbit . . . "

They all laughed a secret-handshake kind of laugh.

What the hell other kind of life had I walked into? What other story had I been missing? I felt jealous. He had another life. Without me. They all did.

"Whew," Peter said, wiping invisible sweat off his forehead. "Good thing you didn't bring Mali with you."

He laughed. John Paul and Gabriella didn't.

On those nights when he visited Gabriella at work and I had no idea, did he come with Mali?

Peter stood up and Gabriella took off her apron. She said something in a low voice about having "top shit." That was all I needed, a "top shit" high to make me even more edgy. But my whole being was running on that feeling you get when your friends are planning to hang out longer than you. And even though I knew I would hate it, hate them, if I stayed, I didn't want to be left out.

"Are you in?" Peter asked me. He looked at me closely. He was trying to tell me that I shouldn't be in, but out. I wasn't really invited.

"Of course I'm in," I said.

Peter still had his parents' car. John Paul and I sat in back. I thought we were going to drive back to the duplex, or even my apartment. I was surprised when we stopped under the Manhattan Bridge, near the river.

"Man," Peter said, leaning back in the driver's seat, pulling some rolling paper out of his pocket. Gabriella watched him roll the joints. I stared out the window at a homeless man covered with tattered blankets. Peter lit the joint and the moment felt pathetically familiar. I passed on the smoke and Peter shook his head like he knew I was going to ruin it.

Peter and Gabriella started to make out in the front seat, which caught me off guard. John Paul and I watched them for a minute. And then he took my hand carefully, started to play with my fingers. I felt queasy. Not because he was touching me, but because I didn't want to be intimate with him in a setting like this: in a car, under the Manhattan Bridge, with Peter in the front seat.

I sighed, annoyed and unsure what to do. Make-out sessions in cars with friends had lost their appeal once I turned seventeen. Gabriella started to make slurping noises and Peter pushed her away, laughing hysterically. He looked at John Paul and me in the back, his eyes resting on our hands.

"Hey, guys," he said. His eyes moved from our hands to me. "What's up? You shy?"

I clenched my teeth. Peter kept grinning.

"Is it the celibacy thing?" he asked.

John Paul looked at Peter. "Stop," he said.

"Once I was making out with this guy in the backseat of a car behind a school," I explained, eyes glued on Peter's face. "The cops showed up, flashed a light in our faces, and told us to get out of the car. They asked if I was a prostitute. The guy said I was his girlfriend, but they didn't believe him, so they made us show them ID. They patted us down, gave me a couple of quick feels, and told us to move on. It was humiliating. So, forgive me if I don't like making out in the back of cars."

Gabriella fixed her clothes and stared straight ahead. Peter stared at me a little longer. And then he looked at John Paul and grinned.

"Want to switch partners?" he asked.

Gabriella rolled her eyes.

"Why don't we just go home?" John Paul said quietly.

"You sure?" Peter asked.

John Paul nodded, still looking down at my hand in his lap. Peter shook his head again, sucked his teeth, and turned around to start the car.

They asked if I wanted to go back to their place or to Gabriella's. I said I wanted to go home. In Brooklyn, John Paul leaned out the window and we kissed good night. I felt nothing. Fear coursed through my body. Was it just anger or something more? I wasn't sure. If John Paul felt the same way, he hid it. He took my hand before I walked away and squeezed it.

Peter visited me at school the following day. He was sitting in the cafeteria around lunchtime, reading a newspaper. If I had been prepared, I would have passed by him. But he surprised me. I stopped walking when I recognized a face that didn't belong to a student or a professor.

He smiled.

A few people passing by the table turned to look at us. They were students, I assumed, who were curious if Professor Beck had a sex life after all.

"What are you doing here?"

He folded his newspaper into a small, perfect square. Something about that annoyed the hell out of me. Then I realized it was the same way John Paul folded his newspaper.

"I was going to go to your office in five minutes." He checked his watch. "You're early."

"You checked my schedule?"

"Yes. And don't you have the cushy life? Only two classes."

"What are you doing here?"

"Do you want to have lunch?" he asked. "I have a couple of hours."

"No."

"You're in the cafeteria," he pointed out. "You must be hungry."

"I was just passing through it."

"Well, you know what? We need to talk."

"Why?"

"You know why."

"We could have talked on the telephone," I said.

"Right. You would have taken my calls."

I probably wouldn't have. "This is not the place."

"Look." He sounded annoyed. "I know you're feeling trapped and confused."

"Maybe you're feeling trapped and confused," I shot back. "This is where I work. Don't bring it here."

He lowered his voice. "You're acting like what we did was dirty."

"Under the circumstances, it was."

He shook his head. "It was what we felt. And while I don't want her to find out about it, I'm not—"

"Please don't say you're not sorry," I cut in. "Because I am. I'm sorry."

His face turned pink. "I wasn't going to say that. I was going to say I'm not ashamed."

"That's worse."

"Oh, come on." He reached out to me and I stepped back. "We've always been good friends."

I laughed, short.

"Now we aren't friends?" he said.

Someone walked by and said hello to me. I sat down next to Peter.

"What you did last night, was that friendship?"

"You caught me off guard," he said. "I was angry."

"Is this something you can live with?" I asked. "Can you really say that it won't eat away at you? I don't think I can look her in the eye until I tell her."

"When do you ever look anyone in the eye?" he snapped, and then he shook his head, sorry. "I mean, you're the one who came to me."

"It takes two," I said.

"I was high. I thought it was over with Gabriella."

"So you were vulnerable?"

"You were going to tell her without even consulting me. I would never do that to you."

"You told them I was busy," I shot back. "You were going to be alone with them."

"Okay. We could mess things up for each other," he conceded. "Why don't we forget it happened?"

I looked away from him and spotted Josh sitting a couple of tables away with a bunch of girls in sweatshirts and tight jeans.

I met his gaze for a minute. I tried to figure out whether or not he'd heard any of the conversation, but I was sure we were too far away. I wanted to hit Peter for being there, for making me forget my surroundings. In school, it was important to remain focused.

"Let me take you to lunch," Peter said. "You can't eat this cafeteria swill."

"That's a great solution to the whole thing," I said. "Let's go to lunch. Let's make this more complicated than it already is."

"I didn't ask you on a date."

"No. But you're here."

"I didn't do anything wrong," he said. "You came to me."

"I know. Why are you saying that?"

"Because of that look you just gave me," he snapped. "*That look.*"

I stared at him as though he'd gone mad. "You want me to look at you longingly?" I asked.

"You know what, Casey? Fuck you."

He stood up, knocking into me as he passed. I could feel the people around me staring, whispering. After a minute someone sat next to me. I knew it was Josh. He put his bag and his coffee on the table.

"Rough day?" he asked.

"Josh." There was anxiety in my voice. "I can't talk to you here."

"Do you scare everyone off who wants to talk to you?"

I looked at him, insulted and angry, and ready for a fight. I expected to see a *student* sitting next to me; a student I could sneer at and tell to get out of my face. But I didn't. I saw Josh. Over a period of several weeks he had become more than a student. I couldn't deny it.

"This doesn't concern you," I said somberly.

"I don't know what you and Peter were talking about, but I can take a guess."

"Why bother?"

"Because I keep thinking about you. And I care about you. And a guy doesn't tell you to go fuck yourself for no reason."

"Look," I began, stuck on the fact that he cared about me. "My life is none of your business."

"You better let somebody in, Casey. You can't keep this wall up for the rest of your life." He stood up, started to walk away, then turned back. "It's also, shit, you not wanting me is about *me*." His voice was hushed and pissed off. "It's not because you're dedicated to John Paul."

"That's not true."

"Then explain it to me," he demanded.

I thought about answering him, and he waited. But I said, "How do you explain your feelings on demand?"

He looked disappointed. "You just do."

"Well, I can't. Especially since my boss is heading this way."

He turned around, nearly colliding with Zabrowski. Zabrowski frowned at him, watched Josh walk away, and then looked at me sternly.

"Beck. Would you stop by my office before your class at five?"

He left. I didn't even have a chance to answer him.

I called Josh from my office because I knew he wasn't home. It's always so much easier to make that call when you expect the answering machine to pick up. I was going to put an end to it. There was too much going on to add uninvited feelings to the madness. What I felt when I was with him, and whenever I saw him, was a fluke. And it was imperative that I explain it to him. On his answering machine.

But the answering machine didn't pick up. A woman did.

She said hello three times and warned me that she was going to dial star sixty-nine.

"I think I have the wrong number," I stuttered. "I'm sorry."

Zabrowski was leaning back in his chair, writing something down on a notepad. I knocked lightly, and without looking up he dropped the notepad in a drawer and slammed it shut.

Gotcha, I thought. A screenplay. Not even Zabrowski had given up hope. I wished that kid Terry from Introduction to Cinema could have seen that.

"Hey," I said, trying to be casual. I wanted to give off the vibe of being relaxed because I felt it was absolutely necessary at that moment.

Zabrowski didn't say anything. He was thinking.

"It's Friday," he said suddenly. "You were in early today."

"I had some exams to grade," I told him. "I'm playing catch-up, actually."

He nodded, thought some more.

"I know what that must have looked like earlier," I said.

Zabrowski didn't have a clue.

"In the cafeteria," I added, digging the ditch deeper.

"Oh." Zabrowski nodded, frowning a little. "Right. That. The students seem to take a liking to you, Beck. I'm glad about that."

"Really?"

He nodded, idly looking at his desk.

"That's why I asked you here." He looked at me again. "Take a seat."

I sat in the cushy leather chair across from him. He pulled out a drawer and put his foot on it.

"Beck." He was lost in thought for a moment.

"Yes?"

"Are you interested in that permanent position we talked about last week?"

That threw me. "Last week? I believe it's been longer than a week."

He waved his hand in the air. "Whatever. Are you interested?"

I didn't know what to say. "Well, I—"

"The kids like you, Beck. And we need young blood in the department. I had my reservations about you at first, but I've been watching you. I like your style. The kids like your style. They're drawn to you."

Oh right, I thought. Drawn to me.

"So what do you say? I'd have to submit your name to the board, but I'm sure the position is yours if you want it."

"Can I think it over?"

He dropped his foot. He didn't look happy. "How much time do you need?"

"How long are you willing to give me?"

Zabrowski laughed, shook his head and pointed a finger at me. "That's your downfall, Beck. You're a procrastinator. We'll have to get you out of that. Give me an answer in two weeks."

"Two weeks?"

He nodded, a slight smile playing on his face. "Two weeks, Beck. Two weeks."

Seventeen

Saturday night is the best night of the week to go to Bobo's, as long as you aren't averse to large crowds and you aren't depressed. If you're depressed, like I was, you'd think Bobo's is the reason why Louis Armstrong and Frank Sinatra sang that song in 1944 about Saturday night being the loneliest night of the week.

The place was packed and everyone was merry. Dock and Ariadne were talking and eating tons of food, despite the fact that Dock was on duty. Bobo's was also very casual on Saturday nights. It wasn't unusual to spot your waitress or host sitting at a table eating with friends.

"Hey," Ariadne said. She didn't seem her usual self.

"Wow." Dock was surprised to see me. "What brings you here?"

My Saturday nights were usually devoted to John Paul, but this Saturday night he said he wanted to stay in. I thought for sure we'd be spending the weekend at my place because Gabriella was back and she'd probably be staying at the duplex. But John Paul sounded tired. He said he'd overlooked a few things at the office and wanted to get some work done at home. We hadn't seen each other since Thursday night. I felt like he was avoiding me.

"Did Mali move back to London yet?" Ariadne asked.

"Not that I know of," I told them.

"There's always prayer," Dock said, holding up his mug of beer and making a toast with Ariadne. "To us all getting rid of extra baggage."

Ariadne turned her attention to him. "What does that mean?"

Dock shrugged and started on another buffalo wing. I poked him in the stomach.

"Dock," I goaded.

He smiled and shook his head, letting us know he wasn't giving any secrets away. "When the time comes for you to know, you will know."

Ariadne smirked. "You're going to dump that stoic bitch and it's about time."

Dock frowned. "What?"

Ariadne and I shared a look that said, *Oops.*

Dock put down his buffalo wing and looked at us seriously. "Is that what you think of her?"

"Why don't we change the subject?" I said delicately.

Dock nodded, his face a wall of stone. "I have to get back to work."

We watched him move through the crowd of people and disappear in back.

"Damn," Ariadne groaned. She looked like she was going to cry and it alarmed me. Ariadne never cried.

"Ariadne? Are you okay?"

She looked at me. She was far off in another world. It'd been weeks since I asked her what was new, if she was dating, if she was thinking about changing careers.

"What's up?"

Ariadne sighed and stared at the food on the table. I watched her, anxious to know what was going on.

"I'm sleeping with a colleague."

I tried not to look as shocked as I was. I didn't want her to close up and decide not to tell me anything. Ariadne rarely felt the need to unload her personal life on her friends. She had Larry.

"Married?" I asked. Most of the men in her department were married.

She nodded, refusing to look at me.

"How long?"

She stared at me, but she wasn't really seeing me.

"It just happened. Recently. Once." She started to bite her nails. "And I liked it. A lot."

"He's married, though," I said, disappointed. "I knew this would happen."

"You knew what would happen?"

"I knew you would meet him, the one you've been waiting for all of these years, and I knew he'd be married. So I just have to say it, okay? Someone got to him first. This is a completely different issue from meeting a man with a girlfriend. This one took a vow."

She leaned forward, looked me directly in the eye, and said, "Her name's Beverly."

"*What?*" It nearly came out as a scream.

"It's a woman. And it's not like I'm a lesbian or anything. It just happened. And she's married, but very unhappy."

"Holy shit." I covered my mouth with my hand, trying really hard not to look shocked. But I didn't do a very good job of it.

Ariadne shook her head. Our eyes locked. And then she didn't look so sad anymore. We started to laugh. We laughed really long and hard. It was the best laugh I had in months.

"You're pulling my leg," I said after a while.

Her eyes widened. "Oh my God. I'm not."

I let it sink in. Ariadne was having an affair with a married woman. Another professor. A married, female professor.

"Oh my God," I said.

Her news really threw me for a loop. And it wasn't that the idea of a bisexual Ariadne shocked me; sometimes I had thought that she might be. It was the fact that we'd spent months shitting on John Paul for being unfaithful and she was having an affair with a married woman.

"Don't you feel guilty?" I asked.

She looked amazed. At herself, not at my question. "No. I don't feel guilty at all. I just needed to get it off my chest. I haven't even told Larry. Are you upset?"

"No, of course not. What if people find out?"

"We're very discreet."

"But how did it happen? How did you know she was into it? How did she know you were?"

Ariadne shrugged. "We didn't plan it. It's all still very shocking to me. She taught Gender Issues last semester, and I'm teaching it this semester."

"You are?"

She nodded. "You really ought to spend more time listening to your friends."

I flushed. She was absolutely right.

"Anyway," she continued. "We talked about getting together to look at her notes."

"You *really* looked at her notes."

"She's unhappy," Ariadne said. "And that isn't to say it's her husband's fault that she's cheating on him. It's just to say, why be unhappy if you don't have to be?"

I looked down. Was that the answer to why people cheated?

"Is that what you believe?" I asked.

She touched my chin and lifted my head so I would see her. "I believe it."

"I don't want you to lose your job over this."

Ariadne stared at me intently. "It's not any riskier than having an affair with one of my students."

"Well, no . . ."

"I saw you in the cafeteria yesterday," she said. "With Josh. That kid was pretty intense."

"Oh?" I wondered if she saw me with Peter, also, but knew she would have mentioned it if she had. "I don't know what brought it on."

"Don't give me that," she said. "You looked like you were very much a part of it yourself."

"Did I?" My voice cracked.

She gave me a slight smile and shook her head. "Tell me."

I couldn't fool her. I was better at fooling myself.

"I think I feel something for him."

Ariadne rolled her eyes heavenward. "You're just admitting that to yourself?"

"Yes." I was offended. "And I'm not even sure if I really feel something, so don't act like you've known all along."

"Okay." She surrendered. "Let's drop it. How are things going with John Paul?"

Just then, a woman with big hair stopped at the table and stared at me rudely. I tried to ignore her.

"Casey Beck?"

"Yes?"

She stuck out her hand and grinned broadly. "Rachel Byrne. We were at Columbia Film together."

Neither the name nor the face rang any bells for me. It was the one thing I'd been good at after college: not keeping in touch.

"How are you?" I asked.

She nodded, still grinning, eyes going over me casually to check if my clothes were more expensive than hers. They weren't.

"You look well," she offered.

I grimaced. I hate that conclusion. "So do you."

I searched my brain for images of the two of us hanging out but couldn't find any. I had nothing to go on. I had no ideas about her.

"What are you doing these days?" she asked.

I hate that question, too.

"Teaching."

Rachel couldn't hide her reaction, which was a retching noise from deep in her throat. "Definitely didn't want to take that tired route." She laughed to cover up the insult.

"What do you do?" Ariadne asked, even though they hadn't been introduced.

Rachel looked at Ariadne and stuck her hand out. "Rachel Byrne."

Ariadne ignored the hand. "Ariadne Cohen."

Rachel wiped her hand on her skirt and turned serious. She looked at me again. "I'm working in the publicity department at a publishing company. It's not so bad." She nodded, trying to convince herself.

Ariadne and I gave each other a look.

"Screw it," Rachel said suddenly. "I'll admit it. I should have moved to L.A."

"Some people make it here," I told her, leaving out the part about me not being one of them.

"Sure. A select few make it in New York. You don't make it here unless someone else wants you to make it here. In L.A. you're a necessity. In New York you need to have what they're looking for. I'm not that type."

I knew what she was talking about. I wasn't that type either.

"Why don't you go out there now?" Ariadne offered, feeling the same sympathy I felt. "You're still young."

"I fell in love with the first guy who said I was what he was looking for." She laughed bitterly. "You take it any way you can, right? Had a kid. I'm a single mom." She laughed again and threw up her arms in despair. "I don't regret the course my life took. I don't regret my kid. But I wish I were writing for television. Don't laugh. I realized too late I would have been good at it. They don't teach you that in school."

"Television?" Usually, I hated when strangers I supposedly knew told me their life stories. But this was different.

She nodded. "I know. Remember how we used to talk about Hollywood and how bad it was for your soul? We were such wannabes back then."

I hadn't considered myself a wannabe. Just smart. Who the hell would ever move to L.A. to become one of *them*? The people who had bottles of water opened for them, who gained respect from the world because they could cry on cue, who spent their days doing the job they wanted to do.

"Did you ever hang out with Mitch McIntyre? Bit of a nerd. Chubby. Freckles."

I shook my head. Didn't sound familiar.

"Well, he went straight to California after he graduated to write for a little show called *Buffy, the Vampire Slayer.*"

"You're kidding."

Rachel nodded. "I hear he's making millions out there, and he's producing his own script."

She took a breather for a second and we all imagined it.

"Okay," Rachel said suddenly. "I have to go. It was good seeing you."

I watched her leave, and then I sat back in my chair and stared at the table. "That was weird."

Ariadne was watching me. When I looked at her, there was a smile on her face.

"What?"

She shook her head. "Nothing."

She said it like she knew what I was thinking, but I knew she didn't. Because I was thinking: television, what an interesting idea.

"It's ironic," I said.

"What?" Ariadne was about to stick a piece of celery in her mouth but stopped.

"Zabrowski offered me a permanent position the other day."

"Get out of here." She grinned. "What did you say?"

"I need to think about it. He gave me two weeks."

"And, are you thinking?"

I shook my head, picking up a buffalo wing and biting into it. It was cold. "Not hard enough."

"Are you leaning toward anything?"

I shrugged. "Taking the job would be like giving in to failure."

"Failure?"

"Yes. It'd be like admitting that I know I won't ever do something better with my life. What's that saying? Those who can't do, teach."

Ariadne looked doubtful. "I teach, too, you know."

I flushed. "I didn't mean you. It's different when you teach film. Do you know how many students Zabrowski has seen make it in Hollywood? The other day I caught him writing a screenplay."

"Do you know how many students I've seen get that great book deal?"

I always forgot Ariadne was writing a book. She hardly talked about it. I shook my head sadly. "No. How many?"

"None," she said. When I looked at her she grinned. "But that's not the point. I go through the same insecurities as you."

"I'm sorry."

She shrugged. "The other day I went to Starbucks before class. I just sat there for an hour, listening to the people who worked there. And it seemed really straightforward. No complications at all. They were laughing and talking about clubs and there wasn't any bullshit. I wanted to get a job there."

"There's bullshit everywhere," I assured her. "You just caught them having a good minute."

"Sometimes good minutes are all you need."

"But most of the time they aren't nearly enough," I said.

Eighteen

After my conversation with Ariadne at Bobo's, I started to think seriously about California. The idea of actually living there. Would it make sense for an almost-thirty-year-old woman to pick up and leave a life in New York to pursue an *entertainment* career on the West Coast? A coast she despised? A coast her parents lived on?

I wasn't sure. I definitely wasn't sure.

On Tuesday I ran into Josh on campus. He'd been missing my class and I'd given up on him. I assumed he was back with his girlfriend, or playing with some other girlfriend, and was too embarrassed to tell me.

He was waiting for me in front of school, on his motorcycle. Sans coffee. Not that I wanted coffee. I was trying to cut down. But if he had a couple of cups of coffee in his hands, it would have meant he was still in his crush stage and there was hope for both of us.

His empty hands and the intense look on his face told me everything I didn't want to count on. He was still in this. And he was in it deeper than he was before. He wasn't giving up.

A few people slowed down to check him out, and I had to admit that he looked damn good on that bike. I waved and kept walking.

He shouted my name. A woman walking ahead turned around and looked at him. I slowed and went back.

Some women might have been blinded by how good he looked in his black leather getup, but not me. Well, maybe for a second. The truth was, I hadn't stopped thinking about him since that day we bumped into Zabrowski.

"Did you call me last Friday?" he asked.

"No," I answered too quickly.

"I don't have your number," he said. "I would have called you back. I was hoping we could talk."

"About?"

"Us."

"Josh, there is no us."

He was unfazed. "I want to explain why she answered my phone."

"I didn't call you." I looked around to make sure no one was listening to us, hearing how poorly I lied to him.

"I don't care who sees us," he said impatiently. "Would you just get on the bike and come with me?"

He held out his helmet, determined. I ignored it.

"I just want you to listen to what I have to say. *Please.* If you get on the bike we'll go someplace and talk."

I shook my head. I wanted to talk. I was dying to know who answered his phone. But I couldn't get on the bike.

"Casey," he pleaded. "Come on."

"I can't get on the bike," I told him. "I—"

He didn't let me finish. He put on the helmet, revved the motorcycle, and rode away.

Zabrowski's secretary gave me the addresses of ten of my students without a second thought. I didn't even have to tell her I wanted to send out personal notes because they'd missed three classes, but I did. I wanted to cover my tracks.

I hadn't come to terms with my feelings for Josh and I wouldn't as long as we kept running into each other at school. There are only so many times you can turn down a guy who looked like Josh without letting it get to you. I wanted to face what I was feeling. I was going to Bay Ridge.

He looked like he'd been sleeping when he answered the door. He didn't invite me in, so I asked if I could "come in and talk." He hesitated, seemed confused. I asked again. Slowly, he stepped aside.

He lived in a one-bedroom railroad apartment. The wood floors were so clean they sparkled and it smelled like Pine-Sol and potpourri. I was impressed.

"What do you want?" he asked, pushing his hands through his hair.

"You haven't been in class," I said.

"No." He didn't offer an explanation.

"You must be racking up the overtime."

"Casey, stop." He sounded annoyed. "You know why I don't go to class."

"You're right. I do."

"Listen," he said. "Priscilla lives here now."

The name Priscilla, and the statement, and the look on his face were enough to clear up the momentary lapse of reason I had slipped into when I walked in there.

"Her boyfriend kicked her out of his apartment a couple of weeks ago. She's been living with me since then."

The sound of his voice made me jump.

"She had nowhere else to go," he explained. "She knocked on my door and I couldn't send her back out there. Her parents live in Montana."

The scenario sounded too familiar for me to believe. I turned to go, but he stood in front of the door.

"We have a lot in common," he said.

"Like what?"

"Mali and Priscilla. We couldn't turn away people who hurt us."

"How do you know Mali hurt me?" I asked, staring at the floor, wanting to be out of there.

"I can tell. And Ariadne told me she did. I asked."

"Thanks, Ariadne," I said.

"I didn't explain it to you because I hoped it would go away," he continued urgently. "I hoped Priscilla would be gone once you accepted how you feel."

I nearly laughed at his confidence. "I should go."

"I slept with her."

"Okay." I held up my hands. It wasn't funny anymore. "I hear you. And that's a lot more than I need to know. Would you move out of my way?"

"I slept with her," he repeated, standing firmly in front of the door. "Partly because I'm still attracted to her."

I grabbed the doorknob. Despite all of his weight against the door I managed to open it. He lost his balance for a second, but was able to push it shut again. Men are so fucking cruel.

"Mainly because I was mad at you," he finished.

I let out a long breath and closed my eyes. *Shit.*

"You should understand that part," he said quietly. "The part about sleeping with someone because you're angry."

I looked at him sharply. "That's low."

He nodded. "I know. But I need you to see me and listen to me."

"I've heard every word you said."

"I'm not in love with her," he continued. "I was. Once. But I don't know her anymore." He paused. "And there's someone else."

I looked down again, closed my eyes, tried to catch my breath. He just stood there watching me, and then he said, "You didn't come here to talk about why I'm missing class, or Priscilla. What do you want?"

There was something in his voice that touched me; it was a vulnerability I hadn't heard from anyone before. Not even from John Paul.

"I want to be held," I said.

Without hesitation he moved forward, took my face in his hands and gave me a tremendous kiss. It stunned me at first, and then I gave in for a minute. But, even though it was good, it seemed to go on longer than it should have. I pulled away.

He was breathing hard, frowning, trying to figure out what it was about me that didn't make sense. It was my fault, I knew. I shouldn't have blurted out the actual thought I was thinking. It's not the smartest thing to do when you don't want immediate results.

"Have dinner with me," he said.

"I thought you weren't going to ask again."

"I lied."

"So you're a liar?"

He leaned against the door, smiled. "I promise if you go to dinner with me it'll be the only lie I ever tell you."

"Okay," I heard myself say. "I'll go to dinner with you."

Nineteen

Nothing was turning out the way it was supposed to. I hadn't gone all the way to Bay Ridge between classes to tell Josh that I wanted him or to be kissed. I went over there to put an end to whatever relationship he had created in his mind. To offer him a chance to drop out of my class and my life without a blemish on his transcript.

His poor, sad excuse for a film professor had come up with a poor, sad excuse to see if he was real. And he was real, which pulled everything further out of perspective and shook it up.

For as long as I'd been teaching, which wasn't terribly long, actually, I'd avoided anything inappropriate with students, colleagues, bosses. True, it wasn't because I held my job in high esteem and respected my students, colleagues, and bosses. I simply didn't want to bring any aspect of that school into my personal life. I thought bringing "work" home was a mistake.

Josh had changed all that before I could stop it.

After my last class, I sat in my office and stared out the window, down Lexington Avenue. It was dark. The traffic lights stretched forever. I was scared. My feelings were so easy and complicated at the same time. And nothing made a lot of sense.

The way I felt was almost like flying.

I always thought there would be that one person who could convince me to get on the plane and go. And I would realize how uncomplicated it was. And then the plane would flip, turning my entire life upside down, and I would be thinking: See, I knew I couldn't trust it.

So, I never let that person in my life, the one who might convince me to fly, and I never took that leap into the world of the Frequent Flyer. And part of me knew other people—the flyers—felt sorry for me. I was really missing something. But the other part of me, the part that allowed John Paul into my life, knew about the chances you just do not take. He took me for this ride that I didn't think I wanted to take again with someone else, someone new. Josh.

Where was Josh when I was his age, single and struggling through college?

I don't know how long I sat there before I picked up the telephone and called him. I thought if he answered I would tell him the truth about why I was afraid to get to know him, to let him in. If she answered, I would hang up. There was no answer. Not even an answering machine.

I called John Paul right after that. The answering machine picked up on the second ring. Peter's voice. Abrupt. "Leave a message."

"Hi. It's me." That was all I said.

The telephone rang less than a minute later. I didn't know what I was going to say.

"Workaholic." It was Ariadne. "What are you still doing there? Meet me at my favorite place in twenty minutes, and then I'll take you to Bobo's and buy you a drink."

Ariadne's favorite place was Sandy's Second Hand, a thrift shop on Ninth Avenue. She was already sifting through a box of two-dollar scarves when I arrived. I hated thrift shops. Everything smelled stale.

"What about this?" she asked when she saw me. She held up a sheer, light blue scarf.

"Cute," I said.

She smiled, folded it over her arm and continued looking.

"How's Beverly?" I asked.

"Good."

I motioned for her to elaborate.

"Not a lot to say," she told me, holding up another scarf. Orange. I shook my head. "Just your average affair between a married, heterosexual woman and her female colleague."

"You aren't calling yourself a heterosexual these days?"

She flashed me a look, did a double take. "You look drained. What's happening with you?"

I shrugged. "Tired."

"Kids wearing you out? Is that why you were in the office so late?"

I hesitated. "I went to see Josh at his apartment earlier."

Ariadne stopped searching and looked at me. "You went to his apartment?"

I nodded.

She grinned.

"I went to tell him to back off, to give him a chance to drop out of my class without failing, and to . . ." I stopped.

Ariadne turned back to the box of scarves, pulled another one out, inspected it, threw it back in. She looked at me again.

"You went all the way to his place to tell him to back off?"

"He doesn't live that far from me."

"Did you have class this morning?" she asked.

"Of course."

She nodded. "You went all the way to his place to tell him to back off?"

"I couldn't have that conversation at school."

"You could have called," she pointed out.

"I wanted to see his face."

"Nice face, right?"

"Attractive," I admitted.

She nodded. I nodded.

"Is he going to back off?" she asked.

"I don't know." I started to remember the kiss and I knew it wasn't a good idea to remember the kiss. It was dangerous. "I'm not sure how we ended it."

"Okay. Then maybe he won't back off. That wouldn't be such a bad thing." She looked at the blue scarf in her hand. "Let's pay for this."

Johnny blew kisses at us when we entered Bobo's. We sat at the bar. Ariadne ordered two margaritas and paid for them.

"How's Beverly?"

"You already asked that," she said. "She's good. Not as interesting as Josh, though. Cuter. Definitely. But not as interesting. Tell me about his home life."

"He lives with his ex-girlfriend."

"Oh." She hunched over her drink, looking disappointed. "He's one of those. They just seem to find you, don't they?"

"Her boyfriend kicked her out and she needed a place to stay."

Ariadne sucked her teeth. "Likely story."

"He doesn't love her."

"Sure."

"He doesn't," I insisted.

"How do you know?"

"I know. I could tell."

Ariadne started to smile. "You're defending him."

"No. I'm explaining."

"No. You're defending him. You like him."

I wondered where this delicate world I was living in came from, the world where I couldn't tell Ariadne the absolute truth.

"I like him," I said. "I think he's sweet and attractive. But I don't trust him."

She nodded like she understood. "What don't you trust about him? His youth?"

"Something like that."

"Well, you're twenty-nine, not eighty-five. And you think he's cute. From what I've seen he has a fantastic fucking body. He knows how to work a hose so he's probably fabulous in bed. And you're not celibate anymore. Are you holding out for Peter again?"

"Not funny," I snapped.

"Sorry."

"I still have a boyfriend, remember?"

She shrugged. "So don't have a boyfriend. Be single, already."

"Why do you want me to hook up with him?"

"Because he's cute and not John Paul. And he has no connection with your friends. That's all he has to be to get my approval. You need newness in your life."

I finished my drink.

"Don't take the permanent position with Zabrowski," Ariadne added. "Quit."

"Okay. I'll get right on that," I said sarcastically.

"I'm serious."

"So am I. If you quit, I'll quit."

She shook her head. "I was thinking about our conversation the other day. You know, the Starbucks thing? Anyway, I don't think you're cut out for teaching. I don't mean that as an insult. It's just, you don't have any friends at work. Your students would rather sleep with you than learn from you. And you really want to write for television."

"No, I don't."

"You didn't see your face that night we bumped into Rachel Byrne. I did. The second she said *Buffy the Vampire Slayer* your face lit up. You love television. You want to write for television."

I hadn't told Ariadne that I was thinking about television a lot since that night we bumped into Rachel. For some reason, it annoyed me that she could read me so well.

"I don't want to write for television," I said.

"So don't write for television." She shrugged.

"Thank you."

"You're welcome. I just thought you should try something new. Get out of New York. No baggage."

"It's not that simple," I said.

Ariadne ordered two more margaritas. Johnny, who had been listening to our entire conversation, talked while he made them. He said, "Time flies."

"It sure does," Ariadne agreed.

"It's scary how time barely exists," he continued in his thick Irish accent. "You want to do something, you gotta do it. No time for indecision."

"Absolutely," Ariadne said.

"You take control of time," Johnny demanded. "You beautiful ladies. You take control of it and don't let anything stand in your way. Otherwise, your opportunities disappear."

"Oh Johnny," I said. "Don't be that bartender. The bartender who knows everything."

Johnny laughed and finished making the margaritas. He placed them in front of us and Ariadne reached in her pocket for cash.

Johnny held up his hand. "It's on the house," he said.

Twenty

On Wednesday night, John Paul and I went to an unfamiliar place near his apartment after dinner. I wanted to try *newness*. The place was dark and crowded and loud. John Paul was uncomfortable the second we walked through the front door, but I couldn't blame him. The man at the door patted us down, saying they wanted to keep the place safe and they did it to everyone. I thought John Paul was going to kick him.

I ordered a margarita and John Paul ordered a whiskey sour. The drinks were weak and expensive.

"Tell me again why you didn't want to go to Maddalena's," he shouted over the music.

"I wanted to go someplace different."

A trio of heavily madeup young women bumped into us, screamed sorry in our ears and giggled. John Paul glared at them.

"You'd think we could just go to Maddalena's for a decent drink after that dinner," he barked.

Dinner had been a disaster. We ate at Suzy's, a small Korean restaurant in the Village that Zabrowski was always recommending. John Paul hated it. He couldn't figure out what anything was and what he ordered was too spicy. He was annoying and childish and I wondered if he'd always been that way and I just ignored it.

I wanted to stay and finish our nine-dollar drinks, but he was happy to leave them at the bar for some poor soul who didn't mind drinking used alcohol. We left, passing several people waiting to be patted down.

Outside John Paul raised his arms in the air and let out a loud yell. He wanted to walk for a while and I knew what that meant. When we passed Maddalena's, he stopped and didn't bother to ask if I wanted to go in. I didn't. I knew Peter and Gabriella would be there. And, since we hadn't even talked about the last time we were together—in the backseat of the car with Peter and Gabriella—I thought we should go back to his place and be alone, mention it. But he was inside before I could stop him.

Peter and Gabriella were standing by the bar with a couple I'd never met. John Paul smiled brightly, asked how they were doing. Peter greeted me coolly. Gabriella kissed my cheek. They forgot to introduce me to the other couple.

John Paul ordered a margarita for me and made some comment about the price and quality. I leaned against the bar behind Gabriella and felt out of place.

"Ready for Saturday?" I asked when the couple left and Gabriella looked at me.

"Yeah. I think so," she said vaguely.

"Do you need any help?"

She tilted her head. "With the party? No. I'm good. Thanks. It's sweet of you to offer."

Sweet of me to offer? "Well, you said you were going to call me. . . ."

"Oh, right." She bit her lip. "I forgot. It's all going smoothly. I invited a lot of people."

Gabriella looked at Peter and he asked if she was ready to go home. She nodded. Peter looked at me. I couldn't read the expression on his face.

John Paul watched them leave and shook his head. "I think they're fighting again."

I hadn't planned to go home. It was late. I didn't feel like spending money on a cab. But John Paul flagged one down for me the minute we left Maddalena's, and I thought: There isn't a reason anymore, is there? If there is, I've lost sight of it and have no idea how to find it again.

"I want to come over," I said.

He stood there, holding the cab door open for me. "What?"

"I want to be with you," I said. "I don't want to go home in a cab."

We stared at each other. The cab driver honked his horn impatiently.

"I want to be with you, too," he said.

"Then why are you being this way? Why are you sending me home in a cab?"

"Being what way?" he asked. "I have a meeting at seven in the morning. I didn't think you'd want to come over since I have to go to bed early."

Slowly, I walked toward the open cab door. We kissed good night, lips touching lightly.

"I'll call you tomorrow," he said.

I nodded, not sure if I believed him, not sure if it mattered.

• • •

The next morning I didn't get out of bed. I called Zabrowski's secretary and asked her to cancel my classes. She suggested I ask someone to cover them, otherwise I'd probably have to make them up. It was close to the end of the semester. I didn't know anyone in my department who would agree to cover me without asking twenty questions, and then treating me like I owed him a blood transfusion, so I called Ariadne. No problem, she said when I reached her at school. As long as I faxed over my lesson plans.

I stayed in bed and watched television all day. I watched shows I loved when I was suffering through high school, like *The Jeffersons* and *Little House on the Prairie*. I became addicted to the new stuff I'd missed when I was in college, like *My So-Called Life*. I laughed my ass off, and a couple of times Claire Danes made me cry. I thought: They really hit it on the head sometimes, don't they? But most of the time I thought: I can write this shit.

I called my mother that evening.

"What's wrong?" Mom said, automatically concerned.

"Just calling to say hi."

"Oh? Everything's okay?"

"Yes." I could hear people in the background and I felt jealous. Mom and Dad were partying it up while I was sitting in their apartment, depressed.

"Is that all?" she asked suspiciously.

"I'm thinking about making a visit when the semester's over," I told her.

"Why?" she asked.

"To see you and Dad. I miss you."

I wasn't ready to admit I was thinking about changing careers and moving out there.

"That would be nice, honey."

"How's Dad?"

Mom sighed. "We have some people over now. We're celebrating. He's doing another documentary in September."

"Good for him."

"Yes. Good for him." She tried to sound light, but I could tell she wasn't happy about it. Another documentary meant Dad would be away from home for several months.

"What's this one about?"

"He's calling it *My Lai*. Vietnam again." She wasn't pleased. Mom called Vietnam Dad's second-class obsession, because he hadn't fought in the war. Only men who were actually there should be so consumed by it, she would say. Part of me agreed with her.

"Maybe I can help him with research if I decide to visit you."

She asked if that was how I wanted to spend my vacation and I said I wasn't sure.

"How's John Paul?" she asked.

Mom and Dad had met John Paul twice and liked him a lot. He was good with parents. He wasn't afraid to talk to them. He especially liked to talk about Vietnam with Dad, which Dad got a kick out of. He asked a lot of questions and made Dad feel like an expert.

"Good."

"What's he going to do if you come?"

"I don't know."

"He doesn't want to come with you?"

"He has to work," I said. "So you don't mind if I come out there?"

"Of course not. When is the semester over? Maybe we can make a plan and do some traveling together. Are you interested in seeing San Francisco? Or the Napa Valley?"

"No. I just want to see you and Dad."

"Oh." She didn't sound like she believed me. "We would love for you to come."

Then Mom called out Dad's name and I could hear the people around her go silent. I closed my eyes and tried to send her a telepathic message not to shout out that I was planning a visit. Everyone at the party would make cooing noises and ask to see me. I pictured Mom making dinner arrangements and lunch dates. I would never have a minute to myself to decide if I could actually handle L.A. The trip would no longer be about relocation; it would be all about suffocation.

"Casey's thinking about visiting us once the semester's over," Mom told Dad quietly. I could hear him breathing hard near the mouthpiece. Dad breathed hard when he had too much to drink.

"I thought she didn't like to fly," Dad said.

"I'll take the train."

"She'll take the train," Mom repeated.

Then Dad started talking about the calls he would put in to friends. We would visit Uncle Pat in San Francisco and I would have a chance to see the notes for *My Lai*. Pat wasn't really my uncle. He was Dad's best friend and director of photography. I reverted into my only-child sulking voice and told her that I still wasn't definite about my visit. I was still only *thinking* about it.

"Well, honey, if you want to make plans, you have to do it now. You can't sit on it if you want decent prices."

"Okay." I didn't want to argue.

"Why don't we talk about it later?" Mom said. "I should get back to the guests."

I sighed.

"I love you, honey," she crooned. "Let me know what you decide."

"Mom!" I shouted into the phone before she hung up.

"Is everything okay?"

"Yeah," I said, a little embarrassed that I sounded so desperate. "I just wanted to ask you something."

"Okay."

"It's about men."

She hesitated. I could hear her take a small breath. "Ask me anything."

She had said the same thing to me when I was eight and had a question about sex. But when I asked her to explain how a girl gets pregnant, she gave me a picture book from the library: *All About Sex.*

"Would you . . . would you stay with a man who cheated on you?" I asked.

Mom didn't say anything for a long time. I imagined Dad waving her over to hear someone's boring anecdote about the latest movie they were working on, and Mom looking pensive, thinking about suggesting I borrow a copy of *Infidelity* from the library.

"That depends," she said.

"On what?"

"Well. It would depend on how much I loved him, and what was at stake if I lost him. It would depend on the circumstances, and if he were truly sorry, and if I really believed he loved me. And it would depend on whether or not he'd taken more away from me than he'd given me."

I played with the telephone cord.

"Did something happen?" she asked.

I looked up at the mirror hanging on the wall near the phone. I stared at my face. It was a sad face. A face that belonged to someone who felt alone. I didn't say anything.

"Are you sure?" she asked my silence.

No, I wanted to say. *I am twenty-nine years old and he is my first. My first real love. And I'm not sure about anything.*

"Honey," Mom said. "Do you want to tell me—"

"No. I have to go," I said. I hung up on my mother and lay on my bed. The problem was, I wasn't sure about anything.

Ariadne called on Saturday morning.

"Okay," she said. "Who the fuck is Vittorio Storaro?"

"I believe he's the cinematographer for *Apocalypse Now.* Why?"

"How do you know that? Why is that piece of information necessary in life?"

"What happened?"

"Your brat students are *so* obnoxious," she said. "Do you want to know how many times I almost told them to shove their film philosophies up their asses? About a hundred times. This isn't UC*fucking*LA."

"I'm sorry."

"So am I. I had to cancel that Elements of Screenwriting yesterday. It just *sounded* arrogant to me. I couldn't handle it at the end of the week."

"I'll make it up at the end of the semester."

"So, how were your days off?" she asked. "Were you sick?"

"Kind of."

"What? Stomach virus?"

"Television," I said.

She hesitated. And then, "What about it?"

"I'm thinking about it. Writing."

After a moment: "*Really?*"

"I'm not sure, but I think I can do it."

"I know you can." She sounded ecstatic.

"I called my mother and told her I may visit them after the semester's finished."

Ariadne cheered. "Good for you. What are you doing tonight? Let's celebrate."

"I'm supposed to go to Peter's birthday party tonight."

She made a clicking noise with her tongue. "Speaking of Peter, I saw Gabriella at the Starbucks on Eighth Street last night. She was with Mali and Polo. When did that happen?"

"Are you sure it was them?"

"Very sure. Why don't you skip the party and meet me at Bobo's?"

I tried to imagine the girls at Starbucks, what they talked about. "No, I have to go to the party," I said.

"You don't ever *have to* do anything," she assured me. "Especially not this."

I thought Ariadne was wrong. I had a strong feeling about it.

Twenty-one

I dressed carefully, mainly because I didn't know what to expect. I thought about not going. I really did. And then I was standing in front of John Paul and Peter's building carrying three bottles of red wine, and wearing a short black dress. The same black dress I wore on our anniversary.

When I arrived the party was in full swing. I could hear the music before the elevator door opened. The hallway was filled with smoke, and there was a strong smell of curry permeating the air.

The door to the duplex opened before I reached it. A woman rushed out, angrily pulling on her coat. A man came out after her.

"Hey, Casey," he said as he passed.

I didn't recognize him.

Gabriella hadn't been kidding when she said she had invited

a lot of people. I sliced through conversations on my way to the kitchen, yet I didn't pass anyone I knew.

I was looking for John Paul, but I spotted Josh near the sink first, fixing a drink. I stopped in my tracks. Even from behind I could tell he looked hot. He wore his black leather jacket and tight black jeans. He had a fantastic body, slender and taut. It was the kind of body Levi's made its jeans for.

He was talking to a woman in a red dress with spaghetti straps. She was doing all of the talking, actually. Josh seemed intent on making his drink. When the woman turned in my direction, I realized she was Mali. She looked stunning in that dress, and her makeup was put on with perfection. That just about knocked me out. I wasn't prepared for it, I guess.

All of a sudden, I felt short. My black dress felt tight and binding. But it was too late to turn back. Mali noticed me. Her eyes went over me coolly and she didn't look impressed. I felt worse. Something told me I should have gone casual. You can never fail with a pair of jeans and a black shirt. She said a couple more things to Josh, and then she moved into the crowd without so much as another glance at me.

I watched Josh finish making his drink. When he turned, he saw me.

"Casey." His smile was big and welcoming. We hadn't seen each other since I had accepted his invitation to dinner. He set his drink on the counter and took one of the bottles of wine that was threatening to slip through my arms and crash to the floor. He stared at me appreciatively, which is always nice, and also a little embarrassing. It made me feel better. "You look beautiful."

"Thanks. How are you?"

"I should be asking you that," he said. "I finally showed up to class and you weren't there. Are you okay?"

"Yes."

"It didn't have anything to do with me, did it? You trying to avoid me?"

I shook my head.

"You don't regret saying yes?" he asked, leaning against a counter.

I saw John Paul. He was upstairs, on the balcony, closing the door to his room. He was the complete opposite of Josh, wearing black dress pants and a crisp white shirt. He stood there for a minute, looking down at the rest of us, scanning the room for familiar faces. He saw me and smiled.

"I can't talk right now," I told Josh and put the other two bottles of wine on the kitchen table, where countless other bottles of alcohol had been placed.

"Okay," he said. "But you can tell me if you're okay."

"I'm okay." I smiled. "I wanted a couple of days to myself."

He nodded. "I understand that."

John Paul came up behind me and kissed me softly on the back of the neck. I turned around.

"Babe," he said, holding out his hand to Josh and nodding solemnly. "How's it going?"

"Okay." Josh didn't smile. He went for his drink, gave me one last look and walked away.

"Your friends are here," John Paul informed me. "Looks like they're having a great time."

He nodded toward Dock and Polo, who were standing nearby.

Dock was moving to the beat of the music, watching the crowd longingly. He wanted to be out there. But Polo had probably threatened to do a jujitsu move on him if he left her side. She was sipping something daintily, looking around the room with a painful smile plastered on her face. When she saw me, her smile disappeared for a split second. God, she was the last person I wanted to talk to. I waved. Dock saw me and headed over.

"Hey, beautiful." He kissed my cheek. Polo kissed my cheek as well. I barely felt her lips. I turned to look at John Paul. He was busy disappearing into the crowd.

"John . . ." I reached out for him. I wanted to bring him back. I didn't want to lose him. But he didn't hear me, and Polo said, "You don't have a drink." She extricated herself from Dock's arm and asked him to get me one.

From the corner of my eye I could see her eyes combing every inch of my body. I looked at her and she smiled. I watched her rub her finger around the rim of her glass and something about that finger annoyed me. *She* annoyed me. I started to walk away.

"We were just saying how long it's been since we've visited here," Polo said.

"But you do know the building," I pointed out.

"Yes. Very well. I have a client here."

I nodded. "Why didn't you invite him? It would have been very convenient for you."

Polo's smile was more like a sneer. *Her.* And "I don't fraternize with clients. I think it's unprofessional. It's a lot like *teaching* in that respect. Though I wouldn't lose my job if I slept with a client."

"Well," I said. "You must be a very special lawyer. House calls on Sunday nights?"

"Mali's here," she observed.

"I know."

She moved closer to me. I half expected her to pull out a knife and plunge it in my belly. "Does she spend a lot of time with John Paul?"

I stared at her, refused to answer.

"I understand what you're going through," she said, undeterred. "Needing comfort at a time like this."

"Excuse me?" I saw Dock coming back with a tall glass of something yellow. Polo backed off. He handed the glass to me and warned that it was a very strong margarita. I thanked him and took a sip. *Very* strong. Exactly what I didn't need.

A couple of minutes later Gabriella greeted us with a pitcher of margaritas. She pushed the pitcher at me and I pushed it back. She frowned.

"Aren't you having a good time?" she asked.

"I just got here. Give me a few minutes."

Her eyes fell on Polo and they stared at each other for a minute. Polo told her how nice she looked. She was wearing a pink and yellow sari that exposed her belly and swept the floor. She wore heavy makeup and thick gold jewelry. Actually, she looked ridiculous.

"You look very nice, too," Gabriella told me. She was staring at my dress, and I couldn't read the expression on her face. It was like she was sizing me up. The way I sized Mali up every time I saw her.

"Thank you," I said.

"Do you want some of this?" Gabriella offered the pitcher of margaritas to me again.

"I have a drink."

"Did you wish Peter a happy birthday?" she asked.

"Not yet," I said. "Soon."

She tugged at my arm. "Let's find him."

Someone put on a DeeLite CD and within seconds people were dancing and being silly, trying to do moves that were outdated for good reason. My arm slipped from Gabriella's grip and she stopped, looked at me.

"What?" she said.

"Where are you taking me?" I asked.

"To see Peter."

"Why?"

She frowned. "Because it's his fucking birthday."

I took a deep breath. She was drunk. Sometimes, Gabriella was not a pleasant drunk. She tapped her fingers against the pitcher while she waited for me to decide to follow her. I stared at her fingers, manicured and clean.

I said, "I'll wish him a happy birthday later."

"Why?" She narrowed her eyes at me. "So you can finish talking to that bitch?"

I frowned. "Do you mean the bitch you were drinking four-dollar coffee with at Starbucks?"

Gabriella put a hand on her hip, spilling some of the margarita on the floor. "You saw us?"

Disappointed that it was true, I shook my head. "Ariadne saw you."

She took her hand from her hip and grasped the pitcher tightly. "She didn't say hello."

"No," I said. "Maybe she didn't want to disturb you."

Gabriella shrugged, looked away from me. "I don't know why not. We probably weren't discussing anything important. Those girls are very shallow."

"I'm surprised you were with them."

"We ran into each other. It happens. No big deal. Are you coming with me to find Peter?"

"No."

Gabriella walked away, in search of her boyfriend, and I felt really strange. I finished the margarita Dock gave me. I had been planning to nurse it because I didn't want to be drunk. But my conversation with Gabriella threw me off a little. And being drunk didn't seem like such a bad idea anymore.

I put the empty glass on a random table and headed for the stairs. I was not happy to see Polo standing there, at the bottom of them.

"Cute," she said when she saw me.

I followed her gaze. She was staring at Josh, who was in her line of vision. He was leaning against a wall, talking to Mali again.

"Interested?" I asked.

She shook her head, unfazed. "Not my type. Yours, maybe?"

I chuckled and pointed to the wine she was drinking. "Mixing drinks. Hope you regret that in the morning."

She ignored me and kept staring at Mali and Josh. "Where does she know him from?"

I didn't answer.

Polo chuckled. "He's cute."

"You said that already."

I could feel her eyes hard on me, but I refused to look at her. "Probably great in bed," she said.

"Probably."

She raised her eyebrows. "Do you know from personal experience?"

I stiffened.

"You know, you really do look great," she told me. "Hoping to get lucky?"

"Nervous?"

She narrowed her eyes and smiled her wooden smile. I walked away.

Parties, whether you're into them or not, get your adrenaline going and anything can happen. Anything. Ariadne was right. I should have stayed home. The only thing surrounding me at the party was negative energy.

I scanned the hordes of people dancing in the living room for a glimpse of John Paul. For a minute, I was hypnotized. It seemed an earthquake could rip through the streets of Manhattan and no one would stop dancing to the loud, thumping rhythm that only sounded like noise in my ears. I felt sorry for the neighbors.

Josh and Mali were dancing with each other. I tried not to stare, but I was filled with jealousy and tequila, so I couldn't help myself. What was he doing with her? Again.

I passed the food table and stopped to try the curry chicken wings.

"This is tasty." A short man was loading food onto his plate.

"Is it?" I said, trying to sound polite.

He leaned in close to me, like he was about to share a secret. "Four words for you: *Curry-in-a-Hurry.* Twenty-third Street. Fantastic."

I stared at him. He smiled warmly, and for the first time that night I felt comforted. I bit into one of the chicken wings.

"Good, right?" he said.

I nodded and grinned. "Like heaven."

He beamed, grabbed a *paratha,* and walked away. Suddenly, I was the one standing by the food table devouring chicken wings, swaying romantically to Puff Daddy's rendition of "Every Breath You Take." My hands were a greasy nightmare.

"You lucky girl."

A very pretty woman was smiling at me.

"What?"

"You and John Paul," she said. "What a catch."

I stared at her, my mouth full. "Who are you?" A piece of

chicken fell out of my mouth. I caught it before it landed on the floor and put it on my plate.

"Jasmine." She stuck out her hand, then pulled it away when she caught a glimpse of mine. She grimaced. "I'm Pete's secretary."

"Pete? I didn't know he had a secretary."

She downed the drink in her hand without flinching.

"Vodka," she said. "Vodka and men. My two weaknesses."

"We all have our vices." I started to feel uncomfortable. I looked around for a napkin.

"But the thing is," she continued, "when I'm feeling nauseous and sad the next day, I never regret the vodka."

She laughed at her own words so I didn't have to. And then she sighed again. I followed her gaze and realized she was staring at my boyfriend. It hadn't occurred to me that John Paul had more than two admirers in the room. I was suddenly angry with her for wanting him right there in front of me, and seeking me out to warn me that I better hold on to him tightly.

I left Jasmine at the food table, washed my hands in the kitchen, grabbed another margarita and headed for him. And then I saw Gabriella and Peter heading my way.

"Happy birthday," I said, giving Peter a kiss on the cheek.

"I don't want to make any more fucking margaritas," Gabriella groaned.

"Don't. You're the only one drinking them," Peter said.

This struck her as funny and she started to laugh hysterically. Then she stopped abruptly and stared at me.

"Why are you looking at him like that?"

Her words materialized in my brain slowly and I realized she was talking to me.

"Who?" I asked.

"My boyfriend."

"I wasn't looking at him," I said carefully.

I could feel a certain amount of panic pass between Peter and me like electric static. Peter put his arm around her. "Babe," he said. "She wasn't looking at me."

Gabriella shrugged his arm off her shoulders and glared at him. "Yes, she was. What are you keeping from me?"

I froze.

Peter pulled back from her as though she'd just hit him and he was contemplating hitting her back. "What the fuck are you talking about?"

"Polo just said this thing to me."

"What thing?" He sounded annoyed.

"She said she admires me. Because I'm so confident about us."

He rolled his eyes and looked around the room. As far as he was concerned, the conversation was over.

"She was talking about you and Casey," Gabriella continued, looking at me. "How well you get along with each other. She admires me because she could never be as cool as I am about your relationship."

Peter looked at me.

"Isn't that funny?" she said. "Because I realized I'm not that cool about it."

"We don't have a relationship," I said.

"Friendship," Gabriella revised.

"Well, Polo is trying to get a rise out of you for some reason," I told Gabriella. "Because her boyfriend is one of my best friends and she's pretty cool about my relationship with him."

"She's not," Gabriella informed me. "She hates it. She thinks you try to influence him. She thinks you have a lot of influence on other women's boyfriends."

"That's not true," I said. "You know that isn't true. Why are you listening to her?"

Anxious to end the conversation, Peter grasped Gabriella's elbow and led her away. "We'll see you, Casey," he said. "I'm going to get another drink."

I went to the bathroom. I avoided the mirror and tried to catch my breath. After a while, someone knocked on the door.

"I'm fine," I said loudly, sounding in control. There was only a slight crack in my voice.

"Great," the voice said. "But are you going to be much longer?"

I came out of the bathroom and smiled at the tall man waiting to use it. He smiled back.

I saw John Paul heading up the stairs to his room. He was with Mali. I started to follow him, but Peter caught my arm.

"What the hell did you say to her?" he barked.

"Me? I didn't say anything."

"Neither did I."

"It was Polo." I watched Mali and John Paul stop in front of his bedroom. They looked like they were arguing.

"Why do you women do this shit to each other?" Peter hissed.

"Oh, men don't do the same thing?" I shot back.

"Let's nip this in the bud now," he said. "Tell Dock to take her home. I have a bad feeling about her."

"I can't ask him to leave."

"He's one of your closest friends, isn't he?"

"This is your party. You ask him to leave."

His eyes focused on something behind me. "Gabriella's coming," he warned.

I escaped to the staircase, too late to witness the argument Mali was having with John Paul. He was gone. Mali was on her

way down. She bumped into me, pretended to be surprised to
see me.

"Little Miss Casey," she said, touching her hand to her chest
like a prim and proper Southern belle. "Don't you look sweet."

"What were you talking about?" I asked.

She looked out into the crowd below. "I guess we could ask
you the same question. What were you talking about with Peter? John Paul was very curious. I managed to divert him."

She started down the stairs. I stuck my foot in front of her.
She tripped, but she did not fall. I caught her just in time, and
she grabbed the banister for extra support. It was a graceful
save. She only looked slightly foolish. After all, she was the
dancer.

"Be careful," I told her loudly. "The margaritas are very
strong. If you're going to continue drinking, you should probably avoid the stairs."

I ran up the rest of the stairs and found John Paul in his
room. He was sitting on his bed, changing into a different pair
of shoes. He looked up and smiled at me.

"You look beautiful tonight," he told me as I walked into the
room and closed the door behind me. "I haven't had a chance
to tell you that."

"Thanks," I said.

He stood up. He was staring at me with love and concern
and . . . desire. I thought it was desire. We started to kiss the
way we used to kiss, and it was beautiful and exhilarating. And
then I was unbuttoning his shirt, saying, "I don't want to lose
you to her." And he was kissing my face, my ears, and my neck.
It was like nothing had ever been wrong with us, until I
reached down and tried to unbutton his pants.

He grabbed my hand.

"What?" I said.

He held my hand, brought it up to his mouth and kissed it. I pushed him down on the bed and sat on his lap. We started to kiss again; his hands caressed my back. I reached out and pulled open his nightstand drawers, searched for the condoms with my free hand.

He pulled away. "What are you doing?" he asked.

"I'm looking for the condoms."

"What condoms?"

I moved off him and looked inside the drawers. "The Avanti condoms," I said. "Golden. Ribbed. The ones we've never used."

He looked alarmed. "What are you talking about? Why do we need condoms?"

I laughed. "Have you forgotten what they're used for already?"

He stared at me like he didn't understand.

"What?" I asked.

He looked into my eyes and said, "Not when there's a party going on underneath us. Anyone could walk in."

"So we'll lock the door."

He stood up slowly and went to the door. He didn't lock it.

"Casey, babe," he said. I hated when he called me babe. Really *hated* it. "I don't own any golden, ribbed condoms. I think colored condoms are obscene."

I closed the drawers. "They're gone," I said. "But you did have them. I saw them."

"When were you going through my things?"

"I wasn't going through your things," I said. "The other day I was looking for Blistex."

He tilted his head, stared at me for a long time. "What other day?" he asked.

"The day I couldn't find you. The day you weren't with Mali."

"If you found some condoms in my drawer," he said slowly,

as though he knew what I was thinking, "they were probably old and I got rid of them."

And then he grinned the grin I loved. Flashed the crooked tooth I adored. It was what he did to everyone when he wanted to charm them, when he wanted them to forget he was simply another human being with flaws. And I knew what it meant. I knew why he was looking at me the way he looked at the waitresses in Maddalena's. It wasn't the first time I knew it. It was the first time I wanted to know it. And all of a sudden, I wanted to be cruel. I was sick of deducing and fretting and never knowing the absolute truth.

"We can do it without condoms," I told him.

I liked seeing the blush develop and darken his skin. I liked the way he lost his cocky smile.

"Honey." He sounded tired. "Look, it's not that I don't want to do it. It's been a long time. Don't you think it should be special? Music, candles, dinner?"

"It has been a long time," I agreed. "And we have tried. We tried music, candles and dinner. It didn't work."

"That wasn't my fault."

"I could argue that," I said.

"What are you doing? Why are you trying to start an argument here? It's a party. Aren't we supposed to be having fun?"

"Where are the condoms?" I asked.

"*Why?* Because you want to have sex?"

"Because I want to know where they are and why they were in your nightstand drawer in the first place."

He took a deep breath. "I am sick to death of this shit, Casey. I can't stand it anymore. You don't trust me."

"I've trusted you."

"You haven't touched me in, I don't know, four months, and *I have bent over backward being patient and understanding,*" he

continued. "And now, at a really inconvenient time, you just decide you want me and I'm supposed to obey? Where's *your* patience and understanding? Maybe I don't want you right now."

We are not close, I thought. There had been signs of closeness. Moments. Of course. Laughter and smiles, kisses and sex
make you feel close to someone. And he had accepted me, little
Miss Casey. He had let me into his world of obsessively ironed
black shirts and pants, and coolness. All the while keeping this
crucial part of himself from me, the part he gave to Mali and
never took back. And I thought, To hell with this. He was
everything I wanted, and in an instant, he wasn't.

I put my hand on the doorknob and turned it.

"Fuck," he said. He reached for me and pulled me into an
embrace. I pushed myself out of his arms.

"I don't know what to say to you," he said. "What do you
want from me?"

*This is what I want. I want to be able to look Gabriella in the
eye. I want my celibacy back. I want Mali to disappear. I want to
be a kid again. I want to be held. I want someone to make love to
me and mean it.*

"I want you to go away," I said.

The color drained from his face and I wanted to comfort
him. But I couldn't. And it wasn't that I didn't feel badly for
him. I did. It was that I had waited so long for him to tell me
what I meant to him, and what she didn't mean, and I had
waited so long to forgive him. And he wanted to take all of the
goodness and patience out of it just because he lived without
sex for a while.

"You mean it?" His voice was hoarse.

"Yes," I whispered. I did.

He moved away from me, stared at me like I was a stranger. I
tried to speak and he shook his head.

"You don't have to say anything," he said.

"I want to."

"You don't have to. Just go."

I didn't go. I couldn't. Not like that. At the same time, there was nothing left to say.

"John Paul—" I tried.

He pushed past me, unable to hear my voice. I didn't turn around. I didn't want to watch him leave.

Minutes later, Mali was standing in the doorway of John Paul's bedroom looking as casual as a jazz musician. I was sitting on his bed, waiting.

"So," she said. "How's it going?"

"Fine."

"You and John Paul okay?"

"Why do you ask?"

"He left the party."

"He's going to buy more beer," I told her.

She laughed and I looked at her. "Good one."

"Would you get out?" I asked softly.

"It's good to get things off your chest," she said. "Sometimes, the person you least expect is the best listener."

"And the least trustworthy. Now, would you please get out?"

She was going to leave. But Gabriella popped her head inside the room. "What's going on? John Paul left. Peter went after him. Are they fighting about something?"

I stood up and walked out of the bedroom. I was going home. But Polo was walking up the stairs and I stopped. My mouth went dry.

"Casey," Gabriella prodded.

I turned around to look at Gabriella again. Polo came up

behind me. She put her hand on my back and pushed me gently. Later, I decided, I'll throw her over the balcony for that.

Gabriella stared at me and waited for an answer to a question I'd missed.

"She knows," Polo barked behind me.

The look on Gabriella's face—wounded, suspicious, con-
fused—answered any questions I might have had about what
Polo thought she knew. I backed away from them and
Gabriella took a deep breath.

"We told you," Polo said to her.

My eyes settled on Mali. The music was pumping loudly,
but all I could hear was Mali breathing. It was fast and deep,
and it filled my ears. She didn't look like a winner. For a second, I thought she looked disappointed.

I was relieved when she walked past me without a word.
Polo looked perplexed as she watched Mali walk down the
stairs. I turned my attention to Gabriella again. She was watching me with those huge, wounded eyes.

"I trusted you," she said.

There are key moments in life when everything is so wrong
you have to tell yourself you're a complete loser. That was it for
me.

I saw Peter and Dock enter the apartment. They said something to Mali as she left. Slowly Peter's eyes traveled up to the
balcony and met mine.

"Gabriella!" he shouted, drowning out the music with his
voice. The sound of him made Gabriella stiffen. Then she ran
inside Peter's bedroom and slammed the door. Peter pushed
his way through the guests and ran up the stairs, into his room.

Dock came up afterward and asked me what was going on.

I stared at him. My beautiful friend Dock who had spent
most of his life dodging the wrong women.

"She . . . " I began, but my voice caught in my throat.

Dock came over to me. "What?"

"Polo," I said. "She decided to take it upon herself to . . . "

Dock looked at his girlfriend. "What?" he repeated.

Polo sucked her teeth. "She isn't Miss Sweet like everyone thinks she is," Polo told him. "She's not the victim."

"What are you talking about?" Dock asked through clenched teeth.

"She has you fooled the most," Polo informed him.

I didn't want to hear any more of it. I ran down the stairs and disappeared inside the mass of Peter's friends. I had enough. I was going home. I crashed into a man and his drinks. The three cups in his hands fell to the floor and he screamed a loud, piercing, feminine scream. All conversation around us stopped. He glared at me with bloodshot eyes and bellowed, *"Watch where you're going, you drunk bitch!"*

I was shocked. I wasn't even drunk. I stood frozen in place, panicked and embarrassed. I asked myself: What the hell are you still doing here?

Josh came over and told the guy to get lost before he kicked his ass. He put his arms around me, asked if I was okay, asked if I wanted to go home. I told him I did.

The party was over.

Josh and I shared a cab home. I rested my head against the window and closed my eyes. He didn't try to talk to me, or comfort me, or touch me. He let me be, and I was grateful for that.

When the cab stopped in front of my building Josh asked if I wanted him to come in. I didn't. He didn't pressure me. He made the cabdriver wait outside my door until I was all the way inside.

Twenty-two

Ariadne stood in my office with two cups of coffee. I stared at the cups.

"You brought me coffee. Does that mean you want to sleep with me?"

She stared at me like I was insane. "I called you all weekend," she said.

"Bad hangover. I still can't believe you brought me coffee."

"Well, I did. Get over it." She sat down, handing me one of the cups and sipping her own. "I got the gist of it from Dock, but I want to hear it from you. Guys never get it right."

"It was awful. I'm sure he told you that."

She nodded. "Yup. He said that."

I played with the cup of coffee on my desk, and I told Ariadne everything that had happened Saturday night at Peter's party. She didn't seem sufficiently shocked or disgusted. She didn't offer consolation when I told her about John Paul.

All she said was "I knew it."

"Don't say 'I knew it.'"

"Well, I did."

I sat back in my chair, depressed. "I'm going to quit my job and move to California."

"Then do it already and stop threatening to."

"I'd be running away," I said.

"If you want to quit and move to California to avoid the rest of your life, then, yes, you're running away. And so what? If you're ready to start living a new life, it doesn't matter why you do it."

"I don't want to be a teacher," I admitted. "I don't think I've ever done anything I really wanted to do."

Ariadne tried to look sympathetic.

"I feel incredibly lonely," I groaned. "I hate being this alone."

"Being alone isn't so bad," she said. "You know, that kid came to see me this morning."

"What kid?"

"The fireman."

"What did he want?"

"You know what he wanted," she said. "He wanted to know what he should do about you."

"What did you say?"

"Nothing. I didn't have any advice. But I'm telling you because, well, his kind of perseverance doesn't come too often."

"I don't trust it," I said.

"Why not?"

"I just don't. He doesn't know me."

"You know, some people just choose the person they want

to love. No questions asked. They just choose and they know and you have to trust it. And someone like you has to ask herself if she wants a guy who loves her because he's sure or a guy who can't make up his mind."

"Or does she want anyone at all."

"That's an option, too," Ariadne said. "The best one, in my opinion. But Josh is awfully cute. And you've had a rough weekend."

I'd had a long, lonely weekend. I spent Sunday in bed feeling sorry for myself. I kept the blinds down and hid under the covers until afternoon. I tried to remember what my life was like before I met John Paul. I had no idea how I would get back to who I was before I became a part of him.

"I won't deal with another girlfriend," I told her, thinking about Priscilla.

"Ex-girlfriend," Ariadne corrected me.

"Ex-girlfriend he's fucking," I corrected back.

"Yes, well." She looked at her nails. "We all make mistakes."

"And what does Larry say about that?"

"Fuck Larry for a minute," she said. "Just because one asshole doesn't know how to treat the woman he loves while his ex is in the room doesn't mean another asshole won't."

"So what are you saying?"

"I'm saying you need to call this fireman and get the goods."

"What if I don't want the goods?"

"If you tell me that you're thinking about becoming celibate again, I will beat the shit out of you."

"I'm not telling you that."

"You haven't thought about your *potential* with that kid at all?"

"Wait a minute. You're the one who put this L.A. idea in my

head in the first place. Now you think I shouldn't go because some fireman is pursuing me?"

She shook her head. "No. I'm saying you should go out and get laid, legitimately, by a very cute fireman who has a thing for you. Never pass up a sure thing when he looks like Josh."

"Thanks for the advice." I didn't sound grateful.

She said, "I'm sorry. I don't mean to be facetious. I only want the best for you."

"Maybe *you* should call Josh and get the goods."

She chuckled. "I would. But it isn't me he wants."

I shook my head.

"You can't be happy unless you try," she told me. She dropped her coffee container in the garbage pail, blew me a kiss, and left.

Zabrowski was in his office. He was eating a sandwich from a bag lunch, which surprised me. I thought he was the eat-out-and-charge-it-to-the-school type.

"There's a lot you don't know about me, Beck," he said, referring to the look on my face. "I make my own lunch every morning, and sometimes I make my own dinner."

I laughed and he looked pleased. He sat back in his chair and wiped his hands on a napkin.

"I hope you're here to tell me you'll be around to discover more of my idiosyncrasies."

"I'm afraid not."

He nodded. He wasn't surprised. "Well, I hope you'll stick around and help us finish out the semester."

"I plan to."

He held out his hand. I shook it.

"Been a pleasure knowing you, Beck. Wish you luck with whatever you do."

He turned back to his sandwich and went on eating his lunch like I wasn't there.

I started out the door, and then I stopped. "Professor Zabrowski?"

Zabrowski looked at me.

"I'm going to Los Angeles. To work on a script."

He raised his eyebrows. "I didn't know you were working on something, Beck."

"Aren't we all." I looked at the drawer he kept his own script in. He pretended not to notice and kept his eyes on me. "I'm wondering if you have any leads on jobs out there, or if you know anyone who might steer me in the right direction."

He stared at me for a long time. I thought he was going to tell me I had some nerve. I never came to meetings, never showed a bit of interest in the department, and now I was quitting and asking for help with another job. I braced myself for his tirade.

"Is your home number still the same?" he asked.

I tried to hide my smile but couldn't. "You know it is."

He smiled, too. "Let me get back to you at the end of the week," he said. "I'll make some calls."

Twenty-three

I left Zabrowski's office wondering if I'd made a huge mistake. I'd quit the first real job I ever had, a job my graduate advisor secured for me. I had no idea if I'd ever be able to find another one.

I walked around my neighborhood for a while. It was raining, but I was in no hurry to return to my empty apartment only to order Chinese food and eat it in front of the television while I pretended to read scripts.

Thunder and lightning motivated me to cut my walk short. And the very moment I walked into my apartment the telephone rang. I thought it was Zabrowski calling with the names and numbers of award-winning screenwriters who were anxious to meet with me once I was in L.A.

"It's Josh," he said.

"Josh." My voice was steady, despite how unsteady I felt.

"You just get in?"

"Just walked in," I said.

"Are you hungry?" he asked.

"I'm about to order something."

"Don't. Let's have dinner tonight."

"I can't."

"You said yes," he reminded me.

"I know. But not tonight."

"Yes, tonight," he insisted.

"I'm exhausted," I said. "I'm sure I wouldn't be good company. Plus, I have work to do."

"I'll pick you up at eight," he told me and hung up.

I stared at the phone. I thought about calling him back and making up some preposterous excuse about why I couldn't have dinner with him. But I started to wash the dishes in my sink. And I gathered up all the magazines I hadn't read in months and dumped them in my parents' bedroom, along with anything else that seemed out of place. I did not have time to mop the floors.

I took a shower and styled my hair and tried on three different outfits before settling on a pair of jeans and a turtleneck. And at ten past eight I was sure he'd changed his mind, or I'd missed something during our conversation and he was waiting for me somewhere, thinking the same thing.

The buzzer rang at a quarter past eight. I opened my front door and waited for him in the hallway. I was going to offer him a drink, and then I decided that wasn't such a great idea.

When he walked off the elevator he smiled. He was carrying a grocery bag, flowers and a bottle of wine. He stopped at the door.

"What's all this?" I asked.

"Dinner," he said.

• • •

We drank the wine while he made spaghetti and salad and told me about nights in the firehouse and losing one of his colleagues to a heart attack. We got really quiet and he shook his head, saying he didn't want the evening to turn too serious.

He said a good fireman is also an excellent cook. He said his colleagues always invited him over on holidays and weekends. Their wives felt sorry for him and treated him like a son. He said the sauce he was making was a favorite with his friends. He was known for making the best spaghetti. He said he was happy I agreed to have dinner with him.

When the sauce was almost finished I set the table and he watched me, smiling. I felt self-conscious and good. It was the first time in a very long time I didn't have to gear up to be with friends. It felt good to be me.

"Tell me about one of your scripts," he said when we were seated at the table.

I shook my head. "Oh yeah. Interesting stuff."

"I want to hear it."

I ate a mouthful of spaghetti and told him it was wonderful. It was. He thanked me, waited.

"I wrote a script about two women . . . " I stopped, shook my head, laughed. "You don't want to hear this."

"No, no, tell me," he urged softly, putting his fork down.

I stared at him, lost my smile. His eyes were so serious, watching me, waiting for me to continue. He picked up the bottle of wine and emptied the rest of it into our glasses. It wasn't Veuve Clicquot, and my apartment had nothing on the Peninsula Hotel, but he was there, listening, *really listening,* to every word I said.

"One of the women has amnesia," I continued. "But she's faking it."

"Why?" he asked, touching my hand.

"Because." My voice felt heavy in my throat. "Because the police think she killed someone and she can't prove that she didn't."

"So it's thriller?" He swallowed hard and covered my hand with his.

"Yes." I looked at our hands. "I like action."

We were quiet for a long time, staring at his hand on my hand. When I looked up, he was already looking at me.

"So, I'm younger than you," he said. "I'm white. I don't make a hell of a lot of money. But I'm so in love with you, I can't get you out of my mind. I think about you constantly. It's crazy, I know. But it's what I can offer you. My love and my undivided attention."

He smiled at his own speech and I didn't know what to say.

"I'm going to kiss you," he said.

He kneeled next to me and kissed me. It was a gentle kiss at first, until he knew I wouldn't push him away. Then it became more intense, a lot like the kiss in his apartment, only longer and less tame because we both knew—were sure—neither one of us was leaving.

It had been a long time since I'd had sex in my own bed. I hadn't thought the next time it happened it would be with Josh. I'd forced myself not to imagine taking off that thermal shirt so many times before.

I kissed his neck and his shoulders as he undressed me. I kissed his back and noticed a tattoo of a sun and moon on his shoulder blade. He lay down, unbuttoned his pants, pulled them off. Then he sat up slightly and unbuttoned my pants. He didn't take his eyes off me.

He wanted to hold me, but his arms around me didn't feel right. I couldn't sleep. John Paul had been the only man I'd slept with for over a year. I was used to his body next to mine, his arms around me in the middle of the night.

I went into the kitchen. I drank water from the tap. I stared into the darkness and concentrated on the strange, metallic taste of the water.

I heard his footsteps and he switched on a light. I squinted at him, annoyed.

"Did something happen?" he asked.

"No. Why?"

"Because you've been tossing."

"Can't sleep."

He tried to hold me again, but I wouldn't let him.

"What?" He was frustrated. "Are you sorry?"

I poured the rest of the water in the sink. "I don't know."

"What does that mean?" He stood close to me, forcing me to see him. "Are you in love with him?"

"Who?"

"John Paul."

"I don't know anymore."

"Is he in love with you?"

"I don't know."

He touched me. He tried to lift my shirt so he could see my body again, but I wouldn't let him.

"Leave him for good," he said. "Really leave him."

"And do what?"

"Get to know me." He moved closer, slipping his hands underneath my shirt and fondling me. "We can take it slow."

"Slow?" I almost laughed.

"Let me stay for a few days. We can do a long weekend."

"What about Priscilla?"

He stopped fondling me and pushed his hands through his hair. "Priscilla was never an issue."

"Do you love her?"

"Not anymore," he said sadly. "I explained that to you."

I touched his face. He stared at me.

"We'll go slow," he promised.

"I'm going to L.A."

I wasn't supposed to notice that he was hurt.

He said, "For good?"

"Maybe. I'm not sure. I should have told you before we went this far."

He opened the refrigerator and took out a carton of orange juice. "I think it's great that you're going. To write?"

"Yes."

"Good," he said. "I'm happy for you."

"Are you?" I tried to touch him again, but he pulled away and went back into the bedroom. I followed him and sat on the bed next to him. "I should have told you sooner."

He raised himself up on his elbows. "I want you to be happy. I want you to have whatever makes you happy. But I want to be a part of it."

We stared at each other for a long time. I wasn't sure if I should believe him.

"I want to be a part of it," he repeated.

"I heard you."

He nodded. "Then why don't we sleep on that?"

• • •

In the morning he went running. He came in wet from rain and sweat. He brought in bagels and a newspaper. I ate while he showered.

He came out of the bathroom in a towel. He sat at the table and ate half of my bagel. I stared at him and I started to imagine spending the entire weekend with him. As soon as we drifted off to a peaceful sleep, someone would start pounding on the door. Josh would get out of bed just as the door burst open. There would be cameras and floodlights, making my skin look washed out on the weekend news. Zabrowski would put on his glasses to get a better look at us. He would shake his head and say, *That's your problem, Beck. You don't have your priorities straight. You should really see a therapist.* And then Josh's mother would rush into the room with a baseball bat.

"What are you thinking about?" he asked.

"What your mother would say if she saw us right now."

He grinned and took another bite of my bagel. "Don't think about that."

"Am I good for you?" I asked. I didn't mean to say it. I was thinking it, and it just came out.

He stopped chewing. "Am I good for you?" he asked back.

"I don't know, actually."

We stared at each other for a long time. After a minute, he smiled. "I don't think it matters."

Twenty-four

I met Ariadne in her office. She wasn't alone.

Beverly wore her hair in thin braids that flowed past her shoulders. She was tiny and trim. My first thought was that she looked too young to be married. And then I concentrated on how close they sat, and how happy Ariadne looked. Ariadne had a beautiful smile. I realized I never paid much attention to it.

They liked each other. They fit well.

"Hey." Ariadne stood up and wiped her hands on her clothes nervously.

Beverly didn't smile. She wore the protective stare of a girl-friend and I wasn't sure how to deal with it.

"I'm Casey." I stuck my hand out. Beverly stood up and shook it. Then she smiled warmly.

"Finally," she said. "Ariadne always talks about you."

I looked at Ariadne. She looked scared. I hadn't realized how much my opinion meant to her.

We uttered cliché after cliché, which is what you have to do to ensure that a first meeting goes smoothly. I concluded that Beverly was sweet and intelligent, and that she would never leave her husband. It was just a feeling I had. But it wasn't important.

As I waited for them to finish whispering their good-byes near the window, fingers dancing lightly over each other's arms, I remembered something Ariadne told me about love and happiness. She said we're all meant to make mistakes, and we're meant to do what it takes to make ourselves happy.

She was right. Where she and Beverly were at that stage in their lives was where they were meant to be. And all that really mattered was that they were doing what they had to do to be happy.

After Beverly left I took the train ticket out of my bag and placed it on Ariadne's desk. She stared at it for a long time, and then she looked at me.

"Oh shit," she said.

"Oh shit," I said back.

She covered her mouth with her hand and looked far off. She picked up her phone and dialed a number.

"Sue? Hey. Ariadne. Can you do me a favor? Can you cover my literature class this evening? I have an emergency in the office. . . . Great." She hung up and touched the ticket on the desk. "One way?"

"Return."

"So you're coming back?"

"I had to buy a return trip in order to get this special deal," I explained. "I can take six weeks to get to California if I want to. I can spend the summer seeing the country."

She nodded, still staring at the ticket.

"It wasn't an easy decision to make," I told her.

"I know."

"Really," I said, holding her gaze. "It wasn't easy."

"What are you trying to tell me?" she asked slowly.

I smiled. "You didn't get a call last night? I mean, I thought you and Josh were becoming best friends."

It dawned on her. "Oh my God," she said. "No wonder you're glowing."

"I'm not glowing."

"You're glowing," she insisted. "I knew he would make you glow."

"Stop it," I said.

She grinned.

"I also started thinking about an idea for a television script," I admitted.

"Cool," she said. "I always knew that one day you would realize you could make yourself happy."

I did want to be happy. For a while I thought being happy meant being with John Paul. I thought it meant finding a new job. But I realized it meant doing what it takes to make myself happy. I had my doubts it would happen for me in California, but I had to start somewhere. Actually, I hadn't ruled out the idea that I'd get off that train in Utah and find what I was looking for.

Well, maybe not Utah.

John Paul was drowning his sorrows in a bottle of red wine at the bar in Maddalena's. I planted myself two people away from him and ordered a beer. He watched me.

We sat at the bar for a long time without speaking. Then

the two men between us paid up and walked away. I sat next to him.

I had never looked a Maddalena's bartender in the eye. I did then. He was young, dark, handsome. He smiled like he remembered me. And when I pointed to John Paul's wine glass he understood my signal. He brought me an empty one.

"I'm thinking of you," I said, taking the bottle from John Paul's hand and pouring some wine into my glass. John Paul still didn't look up. "I'm thinking of good things, like the time you first really noticed me at this bar. You smiled, and your eyes lit up like you were recognizing someone you hadn't seen in years, someone you were looking for."

"Yeah." His voice was soft. "It was like that."

"I'm thinking of the first time we ate lobster together. You had to—"

"Crack the claws for you and dip the meat in butter."

I nodded. "I'm thinking of how—"

"I finish your sentences."

I shook my head. "No. That was always Peter and Gabriella who finished each other's sentences."

"No." His voice cracked. "That was us."

"Two people aren't meant to be one," I said. "You used to tell me that."

"I did."

"Remember that day we skipped work and went to the beach in Coney Island?" I asked. "It was crowded with people, and we asked someone to take our picture."

"I still have it."

I finished the wine in my glass.

"I never thought we'd end like this," he said.

"Neither did I."

"I'm sorry," he said.

He stood up and put his arms around me. He kissed me softly and I remembered the taste of his lips, missed it. He pulled away slowly. "Let me take you out to dinner. Wherever you want to go."

I remembered a conversation Mali and I had. She told me John Paul took her to dinner the night they broke up. They saw each other every night for three months. They weren't together, but they were never apart.

"No, thanks," I said. "I already ate with Ariadne."

He looked disappointed.

"Once I thought your love was unconditional," he said. "I thought you'd always be around."

"Around?" I repeated.

"Yes." He looked at me. "Around."

It was the same thing Peter had said to me when Gabriella broke up with him. I wondered: Did they do that? Did they rehearse lines with each other?

John Paul excused himself to go to the rest room. I've never been good at good-byes, so I left.

I was glad no one had told him about Peter. It was something he didn't need to know. I thought he needed a best friend more than he needed to know the truth.

Coming home from work one night I spotted Mali on my train. We both got off at Seventh Avenue in Brooklyn. I walked slowly, letting her get far ahead. As she disappeared up the stairs to street level, I chose to walk through the underpass that would take me across the street. As luck would have it, Mali and I bumped into each other on the sidewalk. She had stopped to buy a slice of pizza and a soda on the corner, and I had just assumed she was gone, somewhere in the direction of Tenth Street.

Her hair was pulled out of her face in a ponytail. I remembered John Paul once said that the best way to tell if a woman is beautiful is to imagine her bald. With her hair pulled back in that ponytail, it was easy for me to imagine Mali bald. She had a big head, and a wide, flat face like a pancake. She was not beautiful.

We weren't going to say anything to each other at first. I don't think either one of us was in the mood to play out the fierce argument we were supposed to have had so long ago. I felt drained. Like it was time to go to bed.

"I heard you're leaving," she said.

"I am," I confessed.

"California?"

"California."

"To live with Mommy and Daddy?"

"To write," I corrected her firmly.

She smirked. "Aren't you a little old to be changing careers?" she asked. "Are you sure you aren't fleeing New York because you don't have any more fight left in you?"

I pointed to the slice of pizza in her hand. "I thought you were lactose intolerant."

"You thought wrong," she said.

"Oh, right." I nodded. "You gave up milk and cheese for dancing. But that doesn't matter now, does it? The difference between you and me is that my success in L.A. may or may not happen. We know you'll never dance again."

She moved toward me. I stepped back. She smelled of rain and earth and whiskey. I thought she was going to hit me. She said, "You never had him. I think, most of the time, he felt sorry for you." And then she walked away.

It seemed like hours passed before I could move from that spot on the sidewalk. A man standing in the pizzeria doorway was watching me.

"You okay, honey?" he called out.

"Yes, thanks," I said, smiling.

Strangely, I felt free. And in that moment, I knew I'd won.

Twenty-five

I was surprised to see Professor Walker standing in my office doorway. He looked dapper in a navy suit, crisp white shirt and burgundy tie. I could tell he felt uncomfortable by the way he kept shifting his weight from one leg to the other.

I watched him, refusing to help him along.

Finally, he said, "I just want to wish you well."

"Thank you."

"Are you moving to California, or is that a rumor?"

I smiled. "I'm making a visit. I'm not sure what comes after that."

For the first time since I'd known him, he smiled at me. "That's the story of everyone's life. At least, everyone in this department."

I nodded, unsure of what else to say. People are strange. They wait until there isn't any point in making amends. Professor Walker started to leave, and then he turned back.

"Someone called for you earlier. She said she'd try again."

I frowned. There was only one person who consistently called me at everyone else's office except my own.

"Would you let me know as soon as she does?" I said, suddenly preoccupied.

Professor Walker left and I stared at the final papers on my desk, all of which had to be read by the end of the coming week. Then I called Ariadne in her office. She wasn't there, so I left a message with the English department's secretary.

I went out for coffee after that. When I returned, the sight of Gabriella sitting at my desk stopped me dead in my tracks. She knew I was standing there, in the doorway, but she didn't look up.

"You were jealous of what we had."

"That isn't true," I said.

"It is. It's true," she insisted.

"I don't think so."

She looked at me. Her eyes were icy and guarded. "Peter told me that he thought you were coming on to him. He told me months before Mali came back to New York. I didn't believe him."

It gave me chills to think Peter was trying to be the victim. "He lied."

"I'm not going to tell John Paul," she said. "Do you want to know why?"

I didn't answer.

"I thought the world of you," she said.

"I know."

"I will never forgive you."

"I know."

"Do you know everything?"

Ariadne was walking down the hallway, heading toward me.

"I made a mistake," I said and Ariadne stopped walking.

"He fucked her," Gabriella stated simply. "That night she didn't come home. It was because he fucked her."

I looked at Ariadne. She leaned against the wall and waited.

"He brought her home to talk, you know," Gabriella continued. "Peter was there. I was there. And I wanted to tell you. But he asked me to stay out of it. I tried to protect you. I tried to be a friend." She stood up. "I hated the idea of you not knowing the truth."

"You know what, Gabriella?" I said, angry. "It doesn't really matter now."

She stormed past me, knocking into my cup of coffee. The top wasn't on tightly, and the coffee spilled all over my jacket. I stared at the light brown liquid dripping from me to the floor.

"Are you okay?" Ariadne asked. She rubbed my back, never taking her eyes off me.

"I'm okay," I said.

"Professor Beck?" A kid with bright red hair and freckles was standing in the doorway.

"What?" Ariadne snapped.

"I work at the switchboard—"

Ariadne glared at him. "Yeah, and?"

"A call came in for you from Tom Reilly."

"I don't know him," I mumbled.

The kid looked at me, confused. "He had a message."

"What is it?" Ariadne asked impatiently.

The kid sighed, unfolding a piece of paper in his hand. "Persichetti was hurt on duty."

I looked up. "What?"

"There was a fire. He fell through a floor or something. He's at Lenox Hill Hospital. The guy said you'd understand."

"Is it serious?"

He shrugged. "The guy didn't say. I have to get back to the office. I would have called, but did you know there's something wrong with your extension? All of your calls go to Professor Walker's office. You should have someone look into that. I can give you the name of the person to call."

Ariadne shooed him away, then she took my hand and squeezed it. "I'll go with you."

I hate hospitals. When I was twenty years old my dad had knee surgery. He was in the hospital for four hours. Mom hung out in the cafeteria, but I wandered around and ended up on the third floor. A resident was talking to a young man who was crying hysterically. There was an older couple with him, looking solemn, patting his back.

I remember standing in the middle of the hallway, watching them, until someone told me I wasn't allowed on that floor. I had to leave. I never knew what news he received that day, but that image of him never left me.

Tom Reilly was a tall man in his forties. He looked a little shocked when I introduced myself to him.

"Persichetti asked me to call the school and try to get word to you," he explained, never looking me in the eye. "You his teacher or something?"

"We're his friends," Ariadne answered for me.

Tom nodded.

"Is it very bad?" I asked.

"He'll be okay."

Josh was in a private room on the twelfth floor. Already, it was crowded with flowers and balloons from fellow firefighters, family and friends. His leg was in a cast, propped up by several pillows. A blanket covered the lower part of his body, and the rest of his body was wrapped in bandages. His eyes were closed and his arms rested at his sides. He looked peaceful, lying there. I didn't want to disturb him.

"You're here," he said weakly, just as I was about to leave.

I pulled a chair over to the bed and sat beside him. "Hey. How ya feeling?"

He motioned to my jacket with his head. I looked down to see coffee stains all over me. He smiled affectionately.

"So, what's wrong with you?" I tried to sound casual.

"Nothing much."

"You'll be on your feet in no time."

"You said it." He tried to sit up, and grimaced. "I'm sorry, Professor. We won't be having any of those late-night study sessions at your place for a while."

It was my turn to grimace.

"Want to meet my mom and my sister?" he asked.

"God, no."

"I told them all about you."

He laughed with difficulty at the expression on my face.

"Just kidding," he said after a minute. "But I will tell them. You will meet them."

I stopped smiling. So did he.

"So you're still going?" he asked.

I nodded, looked out the window.

After a minute he said, "When you used to hang out at the Polka Dot, everyone always said you looked sad. I didn't think so."

"What did you think?" I asked, looking at him again.

"I thought you looked content." He shook his head. "That sounds stupid."

"No. I think when I had my moments at the Polka Dot I was content."

"I thought you were content because you were alone," he said.

"Really?"

"I wanted to talk to you so badly," he admitted. "But I couldn't. I mean, it's pretty obvious that your students irritate you."

"Is it?"

He nodded. "And I didn't want to be that guy, the one who irritated you. So I watched you, and I used to think about Priscilla and me and how there's this cycle. When we're with someone, we spend all of this energy trying to make it work. And then we spend all of this energy trying to end it when we realize it doesn't work. And then we're free, and the whole process of finding someone new starts all over again. And during all of that time, we were only truly happy when we were alone. And I didn't want that part to end for you. Because I thought you were alone."

I could feel my eyes start to water so I looked down. I wanted to find that part of me. The part that was truly happy before I met John Paul. Because it existed. I knew it did.

I looked at the arm that was bandaged. I could see the red sores seeping out at his wrist.

"I didn't say all of that so that you'd go," he said. "I just thought I'd give you an idea of what I was thinking."

"What made you come to me in the diner that day?" I asked.

"I didn't want to miss class."

"Tell me the truth."

"I followed you."

"You followed me?"

"I knew you'd be at the Polka Dot, and then you left. So we followed you. In the fire truck."

I imagined walking down the street, oblivious to the big red fire engine creeping alongside of me. "Why?" I asked.

"Because I liked you," he said simply. "I still like you. A lot."

I sat with that for a minute. Appreciated it. "Thanks."

"And I know things don't happen for you if you don't try to make them happen. If you aren't willing to fail."

There was a knock on the door. A pretty young resident was standing in the doorway with a bedpan.

"Stay," he said.

Briefly, I considered it. There was something about him lying there, battered and bandaged, that wasn't so threatening anymore. I thought: What if I'm not meant to be alone? And then I reconsidered. I thought about Gabriella in my office, desperate to give me the bad news about John Paul. I thought about John Paul and Mali. Maybe being alone was exactly what I needed.

The look on my face, and the silence, told him everything. He knew I wasn't going to give in. It was time for me to leave. I stood up and kissed him on the cheek.

"I'm letting you go," he whispered in my ear. "But only for now."

Twenty-six

We were sitting at the coveted table near the window. We had finished one pitcher of margaritas and were working on the second. We laughed at Dock's description of the look on Polo's face when he dumped her. We shouldn't have. There was still the pain of loss in his voice.

"I called her twice," he admitted. "She screened the calls. She'll never forgive me for accusing her of telling Gabriella about you and Peter. How many times have you called John Paul?"

"Zero." I shaped an O with my thumb and pointer finger and held it over my eye.

"You're a lot stronger than I am, I guess."

"I don't know," I said, thinking about Josh. "I had backup."

He shrugged. "It probably has nothing to do with strength anyway."

"It's just hard to . . . let go," I said sympathetically. Dock chuckled. Suddenly, I was very depressed. Alcohol is good for that: causing sudden bouts of depression.

Ariadne looked at me. "There will be so many other people in your life," she told me. "In L.A."

"I know."

She stood up and went to the bar. Johnny handed her three shot glasses and the bottle of whiskey he kept stashed under the register for special occasions. Ariadne set the whiskey and the glasses on the table.

"I'm not wild about whiskey," I said softly.

She poured the whiskey into the glasses.

I stared at the shot, and she stared at me. Then she lifted her glass and held it up.

"To L.A."

Dock and I held up our glasses as well.

"To Mali," I added.

"What?" Ariadne put her shot down.

"I realized something."

"What?"

"Mali returned to set me free."

I thought they would laugh, but they didn't. Ariadne drank her shot. So did Dock.

"He never loved me," I said seriously. "Not even when he decided that he did. From day one he knew he would never love anyone else but her. And she came back to tell me that in her own way."

"A shitty way," Ariadne replied.

"Yeah," I agreed. "But it was her way of looking out for me."

"Do you really believe that?"

I nodded. "I do."

"So you don't hate her anymore?" Dock asked.

I glanced at Ariadne. "I don't think I'll ever really like her as a person," I admitted. "But, no, I don't hate her."

We were quiet for a while. I guessed we were all remembering some very specific things we couldn't share with each other.

I was thinking about how random love is. I was thinking about how hard it is to know why two people meet and fall in love. I was thinking how beautiful Polo looked standing in the doorway of Bobo's, watching us.

Dock stood up. Ariadne took his hand for moral support and I just loved her for that. It was something I would never have had the balls to do.

Polo didn't move. She was like a statuesque goddess with eyes of stone. And it seemed like forever passed before Dock said, "Would you ladies excuse me?"

He headed toward the kitchen.

Polo opened her mouth slightly, and then she glanced at me and Ariadne. Ariadne held up her glass. Polo turned away and disappeared outside.

When I looked at Ariadne, her glass was still in the air, waiting for me.

"A toast," she said.

I lifted my glass. "To Dock."

"And to Mali," she added.

I didn't make any arrangements for the apartment, so Ariadne agreed to house-sit for the entire summer. Realistically, I didn't know if I could stay in L.A. for the rest of my life. I liked winter. And I liked subways. I loved Brooklyn. And I loved Johnny's margaritas at Bobo's.

Zabrowski called to say he knew a couple of faculty members at UCLA. And then he gave me David Sims's number. He said, "Why don't you ask him to look at one of your scripts?"

Ariadne and Dock came to my place early and we ate lunch together. They bought me a travel guide and babbled on and on about what sights I had to see and what sights I had to miss.

"And most importantly," Ariadne warned, "don't get out there in Middle-fucking-America and have random sex. Wait until you get to L.A."

"I'll try and remember that."

Dock took my hand and kissed it gently. "I'm going to miss you terribly."

"Same here." My eyes started to ache. "Do you have any words of wisdom for me about writing a killer television script?"

"Yes," he said. "Write it."

I smiled.

"If you decide to stay out there," Ariadne said, "will you promise, right now, to return for our thirtieth birthdays? I can't turn thirty without you."

"I promise," I said without hesitation.

We did a group hug, which was kind of silly since they were taking me to the station.

"I'm not good at this," I choked. "So let's go."

The telephone rang when we reached the door. We stopped in the doorway and listened. After three rings Dock looked at me.

"Want me to answer it?" he asked. "It could be your mother."

I shook my head. I knew it wasn't my mother. I just had that feeling.

"Let it ring," I said.

About the Author

KAREN V. SIPLIN has a degree in film production from
CUNY's Hunter College. She is a member of the John Oliver
Killens Writers Workshop and New York Celebrity Assistants.
She lives in Brooklyn, New York